*You are cordially invited to...*

*Honor thy pledge*

*to the*

*Miami Confidential Agency*

Do you hereby swear to uphold
the law to the best of your ability...

To maintain the level of integrity of this agency
by your compassion for victims, loyalty to your
brothers and sisters and courage under fire...

To hold all information and identities
in the strictest confidence...

Or die before breaking the code?

# MALLORY KANE

# COVERT MAKEOVER

**HARLEQUIN**®

TORONTO • NEW YORK • LONDON
AMSTERDAM • PARIS • SYDNEY • HAMBURG
STOCKHOLM • ATHENS • TOKYO • MILAN • MADRID
PRAGUE • WARSAW • BUDAPEST • AUCKLAND

To Allison, who gave me such great characters to work with,
and to the other ladies involved in Miami Confidential.
This was fun!

ACKNOWLEDGMENTS:
Special thanks and acknowledgment are given to
Mallory Kane for her contribution
to the MIAMI CONFIDENTIAL miniseries.

ISBN-13: 978-0-373-22927-7
ISBN-10: 0-373-22927-5

COVERT MAKEOVER

## ABOUT THE AUTHOR

Mallory Kane took early retirement from her position as assistant chief of pharmacy at a large metropolitan medical center to pursue her other loves, writing and art. She has published and won awards for science fiction and fantasy as well as romance. Mallory credits her love of books to her mother, who taught her that books are a precious resource and should be treated with loving respect. Her grandfather and her father were both steeped in the Southern tradition of oral history, and could hold an audience spellbound with their storytelling skills. Mallory aspires to be as good a storyteller as her father. She loves romantic suspense with dangerous heroes and dauntless heroines. She is also fascinated by story ideas that explore the infinite capacity of the brain to adapt and develop higher skills.

Mallory lives in Mississippi with her husband and their cat. She would be delighted to hear from readers. You can write to her c/o Harlequin Books, 233 Broadway, Suite 1001, New York, NY 10279.

## Books by Mallory Kane

HARLEQUIN INTRIGUE

*Ultimate Agents

# CAST OF CHARACTERS

**Sophie Brooks**—This Miami Confidential agent knows how to defend herself against a deadly enemy, but knows nothing about love.

**Sean Majors**—As chief of security for prominent businessman Carlos Botero, he's very good at his job. But to rescue his boss's kidnapped daughter, this single dad will also have to risk his heart.

**Michaela Majors**—Sean's daughter is his reason for living, and she wraps Sophie's heart around her tiny fingers, too. But because of Michaela, Sophie knows she and Sean can never have a future.

**Carlos Botero**—Will the wealthy businessman's debilitating stroke prevent him from ever seeing his daughter again?

**Sonya Botero**—The kidnapping of the heiress has raised more questions than answers for the agents at Miami Confidential, especially when the ransom drop goes awry.

**Rachel Brennan**—Unflappable Rachel runs Weddings Your Way and Miami Confidential with a kid-gloved iron fist.

**Craig Johnson**—Hired by Sean Majors himself, this security agent for the Botero family was driving the limo the day Sonya was kidnapped. Was he involved in the kidnapping?

**Rafe Montoya**—Chief of security for Weddings Your Way, the legitimate business that's a cover for Miami Confidential, he and Sean clash from the beginning.

**Jose Fuentes**—The unassuming custodian at the hospital seems to be nearby each time there is an attempt on Sophie's life. Who is he really working for?

# Chapter One

Sophie Brooks uncrossed her legs and tugged on her skirt hem as she watched her boss pace across the state-of-the-art kitchen of the lavish art deco home that housed Weddings Your Way. Rachel Brennan's soft linen dress swirled around her legs each time she turned. As soon as she'd walked in the door this morning, Sophie had seen that the beautiful, black-haired head of Miami Confidential was agitated.

Rachel snapped her cell phone shut and held her iced latte against her temple. "Mornings like this, I really miss Colorado. How can it be one hundred percent humidity?" Her sharp gaze lit on Sophie's black-stockinged knees. "I swear, Sophie, I would melt like the Wicked Witch of the West if I dressed like you."

Sophie gave a taut little smile and recrossed her legs. "I guess you can take the girl out of New York—"

Rachel snorted and took a long swallow of her drink, then looked in turn at the other members of the team seated at the table. "That was the hospital. Sonya Botero's limo driver has regained consciousness, but

Sean Majors, Botero's chief of security, has given the hospital staff instructions not to allow any visitors until he has a chance to question him."

Rafe Montoya slapped the table with his palm. "Has he still got a twenty-four-hour guard on Johnson's room? I don't like it. Majors is holding too tight a rein over that guy. We know Craig Johnson is connected to Sonya's kidnapping. What's Majors trying to hide?"

Rachel pushed her hair back from her face. "I think he's just smarting over the fact that it was his man who allowed Sonya to be kidnapped. And he has a right to protect his employee. Let's wait. He's been cooperative so far."

"He hasn't heard anything more from the kidnappers?" Julia Garcia asked.

"He didn't say."

"So we still don't have a time or place for the ransom drop?"

Sophie heard the concern in Julia's voice. She'd been friends with Sonya Botero for years. She was understandably shaken by her friend's disappearance.

When Rachel didn't answer immediately, Sophie spoke. "You think we may not hear anything else, don't you?"

Everyone's head turned toward her and she saw on their faces that she'd voiced their fears. "That maybe they don't want anything except to torture her fiancé. If her kidnapping turns out to be part of the effort to stop Juan DeLeon from curbing the drug trade in Ladera, we're going to have trouble doing anything from here. And their legislature goes into session within a few weeks."

Samantha Peters sat forward. She adjusted her tortoise-shell glasses on her pert nose. "But there's another consideration. What about Juan's nutty ex-wife? Anyone of her family could be behind this. After all, they all have connections with the drug trade."

Sophie shook her head. "Why would they act now? They've had years to take revenge on Juan."

"But now he's more powerful. The bills he's sponsoring will affect their livelihood, too."

Rachel tossed her empty cup into the trash, frowning. "I know it's frustrating that we can't seem to nail down enough specific information to go on. And Sophie's right, we're limited in what we can do from here. One thing's for certain. We operate on the belief that Sonya is still alive. And everything we do must be aimed at bringing her back safely." Her brows knit together in a frown.

"And we've heard nothing else from the police, although that's probably a good thing," Rafe commented.

"True. I'd rather keep Miami P.D. out of it as much as possible. In fact—" Rachel glanced at her watch "—I have a meeting with the commissioner this afternoon to address that very issue. So far we've been successful in keeping this out of the public eye, and of course the commissioner is being cooperative with the Confidential Agency, but the media is beginning to buzz about Juan DeLeon's presence here and Sonya's conspicuous absence from her usual social and charitable functions."

Sophie checked her watch. She had an appointment with a new client. Weddings Your Way was a very successful wedding planning salon, which provided the perfect cover for Rachel Brennan's Miami Confidential team. "I apologize, Rachel, but my client will be here in a few minutes."

Rachel nodded. "Fine. Go ahead. We certainly don't want to neglect any of our brides, or make them suspicious."

Sophie heard the front door bell jingle downstairs. She stood and straightened her black silk gabardine skirt. "There's my client. As soon as I can get her approval of my design for her wedding invitations and get her out of here, I'll touch base with my CIA contacts, find out if there's any chatter about Ladera, or activity off the coast."

"Good. Thanks, everyone."

Sophie descended the curved marble staircase, her sleek black pumps clicking. She put on a cool smile and greeted the young debutante whose biggest problem of the day was whether to use white, ivory, or pale lilac for her wedding invitations.

SEAN MAJORS ground one fist into the other palm as he watched his boss being wheeled into the large, darkly paneled study of his fortified estate. He didn't look forward to the next few minutes. He had good news for Carlos, but he also had some very disturbing news as well.

Carlos Botero had been a big, handsome, vital man until a few weeks ago, when his only daughter Sonya had been kidnapped. Now he seemed shrunken, dried-up. A stroke suffered on the day a vague and threatening ransom note had been delivered had sucked all the vitality out of him. Carlos's brain was still sharp, but physically, he was a mere shell of his former self and deteriorating daily.

Carlos waved a hand weakly, shooing the male nurse out of the room. The nurse sent Sean a look and Sean nodded slightly. Javier would be right outside if Sean needed him.

"Mr. Botero, I have some good news."

Carlos turned pale. "Sonya?"

Sean winced. "No, sir, not Sonya. I'm sorry." He should have played it differently, should have been more considerate. But two significant events had occurred within the past twenty minutes and Sean's brain was racing with plans and concerns.

"Craig Johnson has regained consciousness."

Carlos sank a bit deeper into his chair. "The only thing good about that news is that now he can be forced to tell the truth about his involvement with my daughter's abduction." Botero's gray eyebrows lifted and his sharp eyes bored into Sean's. "Find out what he did."

Sean nodded and dropped his gaze. Carlos was no fool. If he knew what Sean was thinking, he'd be even more upset. Sean hadn't yet revealed to Sonya's father that Johnson had been overheard by a member of the Weddings Your Way staff making a telephone call, a call that was traced to a number in Ladera.

"I plan to, sir. I've left word with my guard not to allow any visitors until I have a chance to talk with him." Sean took a deep breath as his gut clenched. "Mr. Botero—"

Carlos sat up. "What is it? You have something else to tell me?"

Sean pulled a plastic bag containing a plain block-printed sheet of paper from his coat pocket. He'd just picked it up from the guard station at the entrance to Carlos's estate.

Sean had been on his way to the hospital to see Johnson when the guard called to say a taxi had delivered the envelope. Sean questioned the guard about the taxi, then called the dispatcher, but she had no record of a delivery to Botero's estate. The guard had written down the cab number, though, so Sean had dispatched a member of his security team to track down the driver and question him.

Sean retrieved the note himself when he arrived and bagged it, even before he read it. He didn't want even the tiniest bit of evidence contaminated.

"Is that a second note?" Carlos asked, his voice thready with excitement.

"Yes, sir."

"Let me see it."

Sean held it out so Carlos's unsteady fingers could grasp it.

WE HOPE YOU HAVE THE TWO MILLION. PLACE THE CASH IN A CLEAR PLASTIC BAG STACKED IN BUNDLES OF 10,000 AMERICAN DOLLARS. WAIT FOR IN-STRUCTIONS. BUT BE WARNED. ONCE YOU HEAR FROM US, YOU WILL HAVE TWO HOURS TO COMPLY. NOT A MOMENT MORE.

"Mr. Botero, it may be time to call in the police or the government—"

"No!" Carlos's hand jerked and the bagged note fluttered to the floor. "No police!" He groped ineffectually for Sean's arm and only succeeded in plucking at the sleeve of his suit.

"The note. It does not mention my daughter."

"No, sir." That worried Sean. It sounded more like a payoff or extortion than a ransom for Sonya's safe return. Sean was afraid the kidnapping and ransom was a ploy to keep Juan DeLeon out of Ladera and distracted about his missing fiancée until the crooked Laderan politicians could shoot down DeLeon's legislative bills.

He was also afraid that Sonya might already be dead. But he would never tell Carlos that. It might kill the old man Sean had come to care about very much during the ten years he'd worked for him. His job was to carry out Carlos's wishes and keep him safe.

Of course he'd been charged with keeping Sonya safe, too, and he'd failed.

"Sir, the country of Ladera is a time bomb. Sonya's kidnapping is almost certainly related to the activities there. The appropriate authorities should be contacted."

Carlos tugged at Sean's sleeve. "No! I care nothing for corrupt politicians. I care only about getting my daughter back. I trust her safety only to you!" Carlos yelled. "Promise me—"

The nurse stuck his head in the door, but Sean waved him away.

"Mr. Botero, I can't tell you how sorry I am—"

"Do not apologize. Just promise me you will leave the authorities out of this. I depend on you."

"I'll do whatever you want done, sir."

Carlos's black eyes burned into Sean's. "I want my daughter back. Sonya is my heart, my only remaining child. I cannot bear to lose her."

Sean patted the older man's hand. "I give you my word as a father that I will do everything in my power to get your daughter back safe and sound."

Carlos relaxed minutely. "Thank you. Thank you. If my old friend Esteban were still alive, he could help you. But now Javier has taken on the additional duties of bodyguard." Carlos took a breath and got choked. He started coughing.

Sean quickly called for the nurse. It pained him to see his robust, vital boss so ill and weak.

After the nurse brought Carlos some water, then wheeled him out, saying it was time for his massage, Sean sat down behind Carlos's massive carved desk and put his head in his hands, replaying for the tenth or the hundredth time what had happened on that day in June when Sonya Botero was abducted in front of Weddings Your Way.

As Botero's chief of security, Sean felt the weight of responsibility on his shoulders. He was the one who had recommended Sonya park her red Porsche and let Craig Johnson, a member of his security team, drive her in her father's limousine.

He'd felt she needed a bodyguard, considering the growing unrest in Ladera and the increased threats against her fiancé, Juan DeLeon. He'd picked Johnson for the job because of his military background. He'd served in some political hotspots.

Now Johnson was still in the hospital from a failed attempt on his life, an innocent client of Weddings Your Way was severely injured, and until just a few minutes ago, no one had heard from the kidnappers since the first note a few days ago.

Sean pictured the original note, with the unidentifiable bloody thumbprint on it and the lock of Sonya's hair in the envelope. The note had been frustratingly terse. *Two million, will be in touch.*

Shaking his head and rubbing the back of his neck, Sean reread the new note. It was scarcely more informative than the first one had been.

*You will have two hours to comply.* Sean picked up the desk phone and called Carlos's personal accountant, who had already begun putting together the two million dollars.

"Winstead, it's Majors. We've received a second note. Is the money ready?"

"It's available. Specifics?" The dour accountant wasted few words.

"No pickup time, yet. Once we hear, we have to be ready in two hours, so I need your assurance that the cash will be ready."

"Denominations?"

"Ten-thousand dollar bills."

"Right."

"Thanks." Sean hung up, feeling helpless. He was used to being in control of a situation. He'd always been aware of Sonya's vulnerability, given her high-profile lifestyle and her well-known charity work. He'd always sent a bodyguard with her to large public functions, although the independent, spoiled heiress hadn't known that.

But the events surrounding her kidnapping didn't feel right to him. From the beginning, Rachel Brennan, the owner of Weddings Your Way, had somehow managed to keep police and FBI involvement to a minimum. Sean had butted heads with her security chief a couple of times already, as well. Rafe Montoya seemed determined to keep Sean out of the loop.

A wedding planning salon with a crack security force. A high-profile kidnapping that hadn't been scooped by the media. And Weddings Your Way employees uncovering vital pieces of information, like the fact that Johnson had called a number in Ladera before someone had sneaked into his hospital room and nearly killed him. It was all too convenient, the way everything seemed connected to the wedding-planning salon.

It didn't add up.

Well, today, all that was about to change. Sean was going to see Rachel Brennan and demand answers. It was time he took control of the situation.

Sean stood and tucked the bagged note into his jacket pocket. He had promised Carlos that he would bring back his daughter safely. *As a father.*

As he headed out into the July Miami sunshine, on his way to the hospital to see Johnson, he thought about Carlos's words. *She is my heart.*

He knew exactly what his boss meant. His mouth

relaxed into a smile as he thought about his three-year-old daughter, Michaela. What would he do if something happened to her? Despite the heat, he shivered and suppressed an anguished groan. *He would die.*

As he patted the note in his pocket, his brain fed him a vision of another note. The note his ex-wife Cindy had left him.

You and the baby are sucking the life out of me. I can't take it anymore. Get a divorce. You can have Michaela. She thinks you're her father anyway.

Those words had pierced his heart with the efficiency of a stiletto. More than two years later, the piercing pain had dulled to an ache, but it hadn't lessened. He rubbed his chest as he climbed into his Mustang convertible and started it, gunning the engine loudly.

How could another man's child wrap his heart around her tiny fingers? How could he feel so consumed with love for her if she wasn't biologically his? He squeezed his eyes shut for an instant.

*It wasn't true.* It couldn't be. Michaela had his eyes, his dogged determination.

His ex-wife's note was just one final cruelty. She'd hurt him in every other way she could. From her point of view, destroying his relationship with *his daughter* would be the perfect final blow.

He pushed thoughts of his ex-wife and her many betrayals out of his mind as he pulled up to the gate and instructed the guard not to let anyone in unless they had prior clearance from him. Not the police. Not a delivery truck. Not anyone.

He drove the several miles to the hospital, and headed straight up to Johnson's room. A quick discussion with the nurse in charge told him Johnson was doing fine now that he'd finally regained consciousness.

The guard he'd placed at Johnson's door rose from his chair.

"Mr. Majors."

Sean nodded. "Morning, Kenner. If you want to grab some coffee, go ahead. Be back in ten minutes."

It was after eight, but the room was still dark. Some morning show was on TV, but Johnson's eyes were closed and one hand worried the oxygen tube inserted in his nose.

Sean stared at the man he'd hired less than a year ago. How in the hell had he been so wrong about him? Fury at himself and at Johnson propelled him across to the windows where he yanked up the blinds.

"Hey!" Johnson shielded his eyes from the bright Miami sun. He coughed and groaned, then squinted. "Mr. Majors." He sank back into the bedclothes, his face suddenly pale.

"Good to see you awake."

Johnson's eyes fluttered. "Somebody tried to kill me."

"I know. What I want to know is why."

A slight shrug told him his employee didn't want to talk. He stepped over to the bed and grabbed Johnson's wrist where the IV tube was inserted.

Johnson squirmed. "Ow. Mr. Majors, you gotta get me out of here."

"I've put a twenty-four-hour guard on your room."

"You don't understand. They'll get to me again. I know it."

"Who got to you?" He squeezed.

Johnson was sweating, grimacing at the pain from the IV catheter pressing into his flesh. Sean didn't care.

"I swear, I don't know. He stabbed me in the chest with a needle while I was asleep. Whatever he shot me with nearly killed me."

"So you didn't see anything."

Johnson quit straining against Sean's grip on his wrist. "You don't believe me. I swear," he coughed again. "The first and last thing I felt was that needle going in." He rubbed his chest with his free hand.

Johnson had been attacked. There was no doubt about that. With a dose of potassium. Whoever had done it knew that injecting potassium straight into the heart would kill a person immediately. But the attempt had failed.

"Why'd you do it, Johnson?"

The young man swallowed. His pale face and the tubes attached to him bore witness to his brush with death. But he was alive, and Sean needed answers.

He waited.

Johnson's eyes fluttered closed and he took a long breath, coughing dryly. "After I started driving Sonya, I got a phone call. They gave me a number. All I was supposed to do was let them know where I drove her. I had no idea they were going to kidnap her—"

"Like hell!" Sean jerked his hand away, afraid his anger might cause him to injure the young man's wrist.

"Look, man. I'm serious. I thought it was the media."

"The media? That's a lie. I've seen the phone records. You called a number in Ladera."

Johnson licked dry lips as his eyes widened. "That was just the one time. Nothing was said."

Sean leaned over the hospital bed. "Don't lie to me again, Johnson. I'll take the guard off, and leave you here on your own. Now what the hell made you do it?"

Johnson's pale face drained completely of color. His eyes darted toward the door. "I got in deep on some gambling debts. When I told the collectors I was driving Sonya, suddenly I got these phone calls. I swear, Mr. Majors—"

A nurse knocked on the half-open door, then stepped into the room. "Mr. Johnson, the lab is here to take you down for your CT scan."

Sean blew out a frustrated breath. Johnson was lying. But Sean didn't have time to question him further. He needed to get over to Weddings Your Way and talk to Rachel Brennan about the second ransom note.

He stepped back from the bed as two hefty young men wheeled in a gurney. Behind them Sean saw his guard.

"I'll talk to you later," he tossed at Johnson as he rounded the gurney and headed out the door.

"Stick with him. Don't let him out of your sight," he muttered as he passed the guard.

The day was growing hot and bright as he headed toward Biscayne Bay, toward the sumptuous offices of Weddings Your Way.

A half hour later, Sean stepped up to the carved

mahogany and beveled glass front entrance to Weddings Your Way. He glanced at the discreetly placed security camera, only one of several positioned strategically around Weddings Your Way. His brain flashed back to the scene that had greeted him the day Sonya was kidnapped. The parking area had been in chaos. There were police detectives, crime-scene personnel and paramedics crawling all over the place. All he'd been able to think about was his boss's missing daughter and his injured security guard.

He had watched the tapes. Frustration swelled in his chest as he thought about how little evidence the police lab had been able to glean from the footage.

The tape showed Botero's white limousine pulling up behind a late model sedan in front of Weddings Your Way. Johnson, dressed in chauffeur livery and obviously not happy about it, opened the rear door for Sonya, who, with her usual exuberant energy, bounced out smiling.

Then, a black limo had pulled up behind Botero's and two men dressed in dark suits leaped out and grabbed Sonya. Johnson reacted immediately, but one of the men coldcocked him.

A well-built young man ran into the frame, straight toward the limo, but the black car had veered and jumped the curb, heading straight for Johnson.

Johnson rolled to one side, out of the frame of the camera as the limo barreled forward and hit a young woman. Sean now knew that the young woman was Caroline Graham and the man who'd rushed the limo was her brother, Alex.

At no time did either of the kidnappers show his face to the camera. It was as if they knew exactly where the blind spots were.

He eyed the state-of-the-art piece of equipment. It was the same brand he'd just purchased for Carlos's estate. Cocking an eyebrow at the lens, he reached for the door handle. Weddings Your Way must be more successful than he realized.

He knew from his own wedding that they were expensive. But that kind of twenty-four-hour security cost more than his apartment rent for a year. Rachel Brennan had upgraded since the kidnapping. Too late for Sonya and Johnson, but smart.

Walking into the elegant reception area of Weddings Your Way was like walking onto the set of a famous Thirties-era movie. A young woman seated behind a delicately carved table greeted him.

"Good morning, sir. Welcome to Weddings Your Way. How may we assist you?"

"Rachel Brennan, please."

The pretty young woman quickly surveyed him, taking in his custom-fitted summer suit and the state of his fingernails and hair.

"Sean Majors, Carlos Botero's chief of security." He handed her his card.

"Oh, of course Mr. Majors." Her cheeks turned faintly pink. "Ms. Brennan is not available. Could I direct you to—" she glanced quickly at a desk calendar "—Ms. Brooks?"

Sean took in the large main salon of Weddings Your Way. *Brooks.* Which one was she?

To the right of the marble staircase, beyond the display of wedding gowns and veils, in a cozy alcove, a tall blonde dressed in black and white with black stockings encasing her long, shapely legs smiled at a petite redhead in bright pink sitting across from her.

As he watched, the two women stood.

*Oh, yeah.* The blonde with the legs was Sophie Brooks. How could he forget those legs? The sleek, sheer black stockings were an endangered species in Miami any time of year. They were extinct during the summer.

As the bride-to-be turned toward the door and the blonde sat and recrossed her legs, Sean admired the long expanse of thigh that was revealed below the short, tight skirt.

"Mr. Majors, I'll let Ms. Brooks know—"

He waved his hand. "I see her."

As he passed the redhead, she smiled pertly at him. He nodded without taking his eyes off Sophie Brooks.

Her straight blond hair hid her face as she wrote something in a leather notebook, then typed a few sentences into a small laptop that sat open on her desk.

Her phone buzzed as he approached. She answered it, listened for an instant, then slid her gaze up his body, giving her head a little toss as she met his eyes. "No, that's fine. I'll take him."

Sean smiled.

She frowned, set the phone down and stood.

He heard the swish of ultrasheer nylon and to his surprise, his body reacted.

*Damn.* What the hell was wrong with him? He was

working, and nothing interfered with his job. Certainly not a beautiful woman. Miami was filled with beautiful women. Besides, he had absolutely no interest in women right now, beautiful or otherwise. He had his job and his daughter. He didn't need anything else.

*But, oh, those silk-clad forever legs.*

With a great deal of effort, he managed to keep his eyes on her face.

She smoothed her hands down her skirt and swallowed, her eyelids flickering. Did she sense the battle that was raging inside him?

*Knock it off, Majors.* His jaw tightened. He was here for one purpose. He had to let Rachel Brennan know about the second ransom note.

"Ms. Brooks?"

"I'm Sophie Brooks," she said, holding out her hand.

He took it briefly. Her fingers were cool, which didn't surprise him. He'd have been surprised if they'd been warm. She was the epitome of cool. Her demeanor was smooth, sophisticated, unflappable, except for that tiny movement of her throat when he'd met her gaze.

"Please sit," she said.

He gestured. "After you." Cursing at himself for his weakness, he stole one last glimpse of her crossing those legs.

She moved an album of wedding invitations from the small table in front of her.

"I need to speak to Rachel Brennan," he said, eyeing the pink slipper chair, then sitting carefully on the edge of it and propping his elbows on his knees.

"Ms. Brennan isn't here. Can I do something for you, Mr. Majors?"

"That depends. Are you familiar with the Botero kidnapping?"

Sophie Brooks's gaze snapped to his, the clear blue of her eyes suddenly turning opaque. He could have sworn something inside her shut down.

She fiddled with the pen she held, then pulled a notepad toward her and began drawing swirling circles and loops on it.

"Yes, of course. An awful thing to have happen right outside our doors," she commented, her eyes on the paper.

*Doodling.* Sean exhaled shortly. "Right. Not to mention how bad it must be for Sonya and her father and the people who were injured," he said dryly.

For a second there, she'd reminded him of his ex-wife, self-absorbed and heartless. But he supposed he was giving the woman too much credit, expecting her to be concerned about someone she may have never even met. She was an employee of a fancy wedding planning salon. It was natural that her biggest concern would be for the reputation of the salon.

But she'd heard the censure in his voice, because her pen stilled and she compressed her lips. "Certainly. I heard your security guard regained consciousness. How is he?"

And he heard the faint hint of disapproval in hers, as if the kidnapping were Johnson's fault and, by association, his. "They're running tests. I'll see him this afternoon."

Her lashes lowered for an instant. "Yes, I understand you've gotten his physician to order no visitors until after you've talked with him."

More disapproval.

"What can I do for you, Mr. Majors?"

Sean assessed her. She appeared to be in complete control—poised, her legs crossed, her back straight. Maybe too straight. She seemed ill at ease. "You design the invitations for Weddings Your Way, right?"

Her throat moved and she blinked.

She was thrown off by his sudden change of subject. Sean made it his business to assess the people he came in contact with. It came in handy. Those tiny reactions told him Sophie Brooks wasn't a hundred percent unflappable.

"Yes," she said evenly. "I help the bride choose the perfect invitation to introduce the most important event in a young woman's life." She paused. "Is that relevant?"

"We've actually met before. You designed the invitations for my wedding."

Sophie did her best not to react. *So that's why he looked so familiar.* She knew she'd seen him before. She'd caught a glimpse of him on the day of Sonya's kidnapping, felt the sense of déjà vu, and thought perhaps his even, rugged features reminded her of a movie star. In the chaos of the tragedy, she'd forgotten about him.

But now she remembered vividly—his athletic, loose-limbed grace, his broad shoulders and lean hips subtly set off by his tailored suit, his nearly perfect features. His wedding to a blond debutante

four years ago had been her first assignment for
Weddings Your Way.

"Of course." She held his gaze. No way was she
going to admit she remembered him after that long. In
truth, his odd teal-colored eyes had fascinated her, as
had his harsh, handsome face and his confident sexuality. She also recalled how much in love he'd been. She
smiled. "How is your wife?"

His eyes changed then, from soft teal blue to the
dark shadows of a storm cloud. "I have no idea," he said
flatly.

Before she could stop herself, she glanced down at
his left hand. No ring. Not even a tan line. "I'm sorry."

"Don't be. It wasn't because of the invitations." His
lips smiled wryly. His eyes didn't.

Sophie sent him a small sad smile. "Nevertheless—"

"When will Ms. Brennan be back?"

*Back to business.* Sophie watched as he deliberately
refocused on his reason for being here. He tensed and
subtly arched his shoulders, then glanced at his watch,
a shadow of worry flickering across his face.

*Something had happened.* Her intuition, honed by
her years with the CIA, kicked in. She tensed.

"It could be quite a while. I assure you, I am authorized to act on her behalf in *any* matter."

He nodded, and his hand moved toward his jacket
pocket. In a calculatedly casual move, he checked it and
rested it on his thigh, instead.

But Sophie noticed. She spotted the corner of a
plastic bag skirting the top edge of the gray silk
pocket. They'd received á note. She leaned forward.

"Mr. Botero has heard from the kidnappers again, hasn't he?"

Sean Majors glanced down at the unbuttoned top of her blouse. His gaze brushed the shadowed area between her breasts like a caress. They tightened in response, and awareness drifted across her skin like the faint touch of fingertips.

His gaze slid up to hers. After a couple of seconds, he looked beyond her. He could have been just looking out the window behind her at the luxurious pool area, but Sophie knew he wasn't. He was making a decision—a decision whether to trust her.

He blinked and leveled his gaze on her again. "Yes."

Sophie's heart slammed against her chest.

*A break at last.* She smoothed her skirt and reminded herself that to him she was just a graphics designer at an upscale wedding-planning business. Still, she *was* in charge while Rachel was gone. She had an obligation to get all the information she could.

"And you're here because Mr. Botero doesn't want the police involved."

"That's right. Mr. Botero has cooperated up to a point. But he refuses to allow them inside his estate. He doesn't want them to know he's heard from the kidnappers. I don't like operating without their knowledge."

"We're willing to cooperate in any way," Sophie said quickly. She couldn't tell him that Rachel, as head of the Confidential Agency, was already working closely with the police commissioner to keep law enforcement and media attention off the Botero kidnapping.

"As I'm sure you know, we've been waiting to hear about the date and time for the drop," she said.

"And your security team is ready?"

"Of course." He assessed her narrowly. She knew what he was thinking. He was Botero's chief of security. He knew all about coordinating surveillance and protection. He also knew all about cooperation with authorities. Luckily so far, he'd barely dealt with the Confidential team directly, and then it had been mostly through Rachel. Sophie knew Rachel had revealed nothing about the true purpose of Weddings Your Way.

He dropped his gaze to her fingers. Aware that she was still doodling, as she did when she was nervous or concentrating, she smoothly covered the paper with her forearm without looking at it.

"So, Mr. Majors, what can Weddings Your Way do for you?"

"I need copies of all your surveillance tapes from the day of the kidnapping. I'd like to interview everyone Sonya spoke with that day. I want to review all the statements from all your employees."

"The police have all that."

He waited.

"All right. Ms. Brennan has copies of everything." Sophie picked up the phone and dialed Samantha's extension. "Samantha, have you got an extra set of copies of everything related to the Botero case—to Sonya's kidnapping?"

"Everything?" Samantha's amused voice said in her ear. "I caught a glimpse of Botero's gorgeous security chief. Lucky you, in charge today. You surely don't mean he's sweet-talked you into giving him *everything?*"

Sophie gripped the phone more tightly and avoided the gorgeous security chief's gaze as her face grew warm. "All the information we provided to the police," she said evenly. She'd never quite picked up the knack the close-knit team had of kidding around, especially in the middle of a serious situation. Her background hadn't been conducive to gentle teasing.

"Ah, okay. Give me twenty minutes. So the unflappable Sophie Brooks didn't fall under the handsome prince's spell."

"No, of course not. Nothing like that." She disconnected, feeling her cheeks turn warm. Silently and fluently, she cursed Samantha for teasing her.

She gave Sean a stiff smile. "We can have that information for you in about twenty minutes. In the meantime, if you'd like, you can talk to our receptionist about arranging to speak with the employees who were here that morning. Or would you prefer to see our chief of security, Rafe Montoya? He's not here right now." He'd gone with Rachel to see the commissioner. "He should be back this afternoon."

Sean glanced at his watch again.

*He didn't have much time.* Sophie couldn't stand it any longer. She had to know about the note.

"The kidnappers gave you a deadline, didn't they? When is the drop? What did the note say? How was it delivered?" Sophie stopped as Majors's brows drew together in a frown and his gaze sharpened.

She backpedaled. "I mean, is Sonya safe? Did the note

say anything about her?" She sat back and forced herself to calm down. Sean Majors had no idea she was a former CIA agent. Her job, and her biggest challenge, was to stay in character. As far as Sean Majors was concerned, she was an employee of Weddings Your Way. Nothing more.

Sean didn't speak.

"Mr. Majors, I assure you that I am authorized to act in full capacity in Ms. Brennan's absence. If you like, I could give her your cell phone number so you can verify it with her."

His face smoothed out a bit as he shook his head. "There was no specific mention of Sonya. But they gave instructions about the money, and said they'd be in touch very soon."

"May I see the note?" She looked at his pocket.

As he pulled out the plastic bag and laid it in front of her, she was momentarily distracted by his hands. They were large and tanned, with long, well-shaped fingers. Good hands. Competent hands.

She forced her attention on to the note, reading it quickly. "Two hours!"

"Right. Not much time. We're going to have to be ready to move."

She held the note up to the light, drawing a curious glance from him. "No watermark," she commented, then gave a small false shrug. "I'm a graphic designer. Mr. Majors, may we keep this?"

"What reason could you possibly have to want the note?"

"Ms. Brennan will want to see it," Sophie said

quickly. "She feels responsible for Sonya Botero's kidnapping. Maybe a copy?"

Majors sent her a suspicious glance. "How can I be assured it won't end up in the hands of the police?"

"As I said, I can have Ms. Brennan speak to you personally."

He shook his head. "One copy, without removing it from the plastic bag."

"Of course. I'll do it myself if you'd like to observe."

He stood, adjusting his cuffs, and picked up the note. He was not going to let it out of his sight for an instant.

Sophie stood as well. "Follow me." She walked quickly up the stairs, her high heels clicking on the marble. Majors walked slightly behind her and she imagined his gaze burning into her back, her behind, her legs. It was an uncomfortable feeling. Disturbing. And yet slightly arousing. Suppressing the urge to slow down and force him into step beside her, she sped up, reaching the second floor and heading straight for the copy machine.

As he watched her like a hawk, she made one photocopy. He reached around her and cleared the machine, then inspected the copy.

"Your confidence in us is underwhelming."

He didn't look up. "This is my boss's only daughter. My loyalty is to him."

"True. I apologize."

He didn't acknowledge her words, just handed her the photocopy and retrieved the original note, tucking it back in his inside jacket pocket. Then he stepped aside to let her precede him down the stairs.

Sophie faced him at the bottom. "Where do you think they'll want to meet for the drop?"

"Who knows. They don't seem to be concerned about being seen in daylight, but they'll want an open space."

"Do it here."

Sean lifted his chin slightly, staring at her as if she'd just confessed.

She'd come on too strong. But she was getting the definite impression he wanted to handle this alone. And she couldn't let that happen. Sonya Botero had been kidnapped right under the nose of Rachel Brennan's Miami Confidential team. Rachel was absolutely determined to get Sonya back, and Sophie and the rest of the team felt the same way. It had happened on their watch. It was their responsibility.

"It's the perfect place," she said quickly. "Sonya was kidnapped here. That means the kidnappers know the area intimately. We can arrange the drop in the circular drive out front. Cancel all appointments for the time frame to ensure that no one is around. It's relatively isolated, yet out in the open. It would make sense."

Sean cocked one brow. "You seem to have all the bases covered. Have you been thinking about this a lot?"

His remark gave her pause. Actually, the thought of using Weddings Your Way for the ransom drop had just occurred to her. "I watch a lot of TV. But it does make sense, doesn't it?"

"Assuming the kidnappers are generous enough to let *us* make that decision, which I doubt will happen. Isn't this Montoya's territory?"

"Yes, but he and Ms. Brennan are out all morning.

That means it could be hours before you could talk with them about arrangements. That's time wasted."

"Who do you suggest to make the drop?"

Sophie took a deep breath. "Me. I work here. I'm sure the kidnappers know all the employees of Weddings Your Way. They would have cased us pretty thoroughly before they planned the kidnapping."

"*Cased* you?"

"Sorry." Sophie smoothed her skirt and looked down. "Like I said, I guess I watch too many cop shows."

"You think?"

She frowned at his sarcastic remark and the storm clouds still darkening his eyes. She challenged him. "You think I can't handle it."

"I'm sure you can. All you'd have to do is walk a few steps and set down a suitcase. My question is why do you want to?"

His voice was harsh, suspicious. He obviously suspected that she had an ulterior motive. Surely he didn't think she was in on the kidnapping?

She couldn't tell him the truth. That as a Miami Confidential agent, she had an obligation to make sure no one else was hurt. If anything happened during the drop, her CIA training ensured that she'd be prepared. She knew how to take care of herself.

Sean crossed his arms, waiting for her answer.

Smiling slyly, she leaned forward again, making sure her shirt gaped artfully. She was rewarded when his gaze flickered downward.

"I love the danger. It's a turn-on."

# Chapter Two

*It's a turn-on.*

For an instant, her words hung between them. Neither of them moved.

Then Sean Majors's eyes darkened and his knuckles whitened against the dark gray of his jacket.

Sophie took a deep breath, willing her face not to express the embarrassment she felt. Her ploy hadn't worked. She never should have tried flirting. Lord knew, she was no good at it.

He uncrossed his arms and shrugged his shoulders, adjusting his jacket as he took a step backward. The set of his strong straight mouth telegraphed his disapproval of her and her suggestion.

She hated this posturing. Hated the idea that she had to resort to such tactics to keep Weddings Your Way's true identity a secret. But she'd started it and now she had to finish. She *had* to ensure that Confidential was involved in the ransom drop.

"You must feel the same way." She stepped forward, letting her gaze drift down to his chest, where a shoulder holster strap showed beneath his jacket. She ran the tip of one fingernail along the edge of the strap, then she met his gaze again and smiled.

"Why else would you be in a job where you carry a gun?"

Sean's mouth compressed into a thin line and his eyes turned black. "My job is to protect. It doesn't turn me on."

His tone chilled her. Still, at least she'd accomplished her purpose. He thought she was a bimbo who had no better sense than to think dealing with kidnappers was a chance for excitement.

Cringing at the censure and contempt in his gaze, Sophie desperately hung on to her false smile.

He buttoned his coat. He was done here.

"All right, Ms. Brooks," he said finally. "Your idea is actually not too bad. It's simple and yet unexpected. So if the kidnappers and Montoya agree, you can have your excitement. But don't forget for one moment that this is deadly serious. One wrong move and you could be killed."

He paused, but she didn't take the bait. She just nodded.

"Remember, we have to be ready within two hours. When the kidnappers contact us again, I'll let Ms. Brennan know immediately."

Sophie didn't realize she'd wiped her palms down her sides until his gaze slid along the buttons of her white silk blouse, over the snug waistband of her skirt, down to the hem and farther. His frown stayed in place, and his entire body exuded disapproval.

She swallowed, suffering his assessment. Probably

wondering how fast she could run if something went wrong with the ransom drop.

"Tell Rachel Brennan to call me."

"Of course. Does she have your number?"

He flipped out a card.

Sophie took it.

He nodded and turned toward the door.

She felt a little dirty, and it surprised her how much it bothered her that he actually believed she'd participate in a ransom drop for kicks.

As she watched him walk away, his grace and self-assurance obvious in his sleek movements, she reviewed his change in attitude toward her. He'd started out neutral, with a little bit of masculine appreciation for her appearance. Now though, he apparently thought she was lower than pond scum.

Odd that it mattered so much what he thought. She didn't even know him.

As she sat back down at her desk, she looked at her notepad. She'd sketched him.

Had he seen it? The sketch was small, but accurate. She turned on her desk lamp to look at it more closely. She'd caught the storms that had gathered in his eyes when he'd spoken of his failed marriage. Looking at the sketch, she noticed there was a subtle difference in how he'd looked then and how he'd looked when she'd been pretending to be a bimbo.

The eyes in her sketch looked sad. Before he left, the sadness had been replaced by distaste.

She held the sketch closer to the light, studying the hint of sadness she'd caught. Did he still love his wife?

Shaking off the question, which was none of her business, she picked up her phone to tell Vicki to co-operate with him in arranging meetings with the staff.

Then she tried to go back to work on her latest assignment, but her curiosity got the better of her. She accessed the archived designs on her laptop. There it was. The Majors/DuVall wedding. Their snow-white invitation had featured two gold-embossed hearts linked together.

She glanced across the salon at him as he spoke with Vicki, then back at her notepad. Pen in hand, she drew two identical hearts, one broken. She swallowed and scratched out the image.

At least that would never happen to her. Not again.

IN A PRIVATE office in an expensive villa overlooking the capital of Ladera, seven men sat around a polished wood table. Three of them smoked cigars. Each of them had a cup of steaming black coffee close at hand.

When the eighth man walked into the room and sat at the head of the table, the other seven sat up straighter. The tall, white-haired man nodded at the servant pouring his coffee.

The servant quickly bowed and exited the room.

"You know why we are here," he addressed the other men.

A rotund middle-aged man lifted a finger. "Is it true that DeLeon's kidnapped fiancée has been traced to Ladera?"

"There are rumors. Someone in the Miami area is investigating her whereabouts."

"And doing a good job of it," another man commented.

The white-haired man pinned him with a dark glance. "Yes. I have it on good authority that the police are staying out of this investigation, nor have federal officials been called in. But that could happen at any moment."

"Who is the contact?"

"That is not your concern. You should be squashing interest in DeLeon's antidrug bills by whatever means necessary while he is preoccupied with the search for his missing fiancée. The Laderan people are counting on the legislature to keep their livelihood from being taken away from them because of DeLeon's crusade. We must continue to paint him as a fanatic, only interested in revenge for his ex-wife's mental illness caused by illegal drugs."

"Juan DeLeon is very popular."

The man sighed and sipped his coffee. "Exactly. That is why I took the chance of bringing you all here at this time. You are my most trusted allies. Before you leave, I need to make sure that each of you understands your role within the next days. DeLeon has several senators poised to demand an immediate vote on two bills, the first to oust legislators found guilty of corruption, and the second to impose term limits."

There was a hushed muttering around the table.

"I expect to hear shortly of a development in Sonya Botero's kidnapping. We must ensure that the votes are timed to coincide. We can't take the chance that DeLeon will return before the vote is taken. Several of DeLeon's allies have vulnerabilities that we can use to our advantage. This is where you come in. Hector, let's start with you. Here's what you must do…."

SEAN SPENT the rest of the morning grilling the employees at Weddings Your Way, including Sophie Brooks. He left with little more information than he'd come with. Then he drove by the hospital to check on Craig Johnson.

He spoke with him briefly, but the young man seemed too medicated to respond much. Sean was suspicious, but the nurses confirmed that he'd been agitated earlier and the doctor on call had ordered a sedative.

Sean spoke briefly with Johnson's physician by phone and let him know that he *had* to speak with Johnson the next day. The physician hired and paid for by Carlos Botero assured Sean that Johnson would be alert the next day.

Sean headed back to his office at the Botero estate and studied the police reports and went over the security tapes. Just as he suspected, he found nothing he hadn't already seen or heard from the police.

By the time he'd finished, it was after six o'clock and there had been no word from the kidnappers. Michaela would be waiting for him. He picked up the intercom phone.

"Javier, a phone call may come in from the kidnappers. If so, let Mr. Botero speak to them, but you patch me through immediately."

"Yes, sir."

"Thanks. Let me speak to Mr. Botero." After a brief pause, Carlos's voice spoke weakly into the phone. "Mr. Botero, do you need me this evening?"

"No, no. Javier will be here, as will Cook. You go on home."

"Thank you, sir. If anyone contacts you, Javier has instructions to patch me through, although I doubt we'll hear from them tonight. I'll see you in the morning."

By the time he got to his apartment off old Route One, it was almost seven. He loosened his tie and undid the top button of his shirt as he rode up in the elevator from the parking garage. He unlocked the door and stepped into his brightly lit living room.

He'd barely had time to shrug out of his jacket and toss it onto a chair before Michaela came running in.

"Daddy, Daddy, Daddy! You're late!"

The blond curls and the wide grin of his precious daughter greeted him like a burst of sunshine after a gloomy day. He dropped to his haunches and held out his arms.

"Hi, sprout. What have you been doing today?"

Michaela giggled as she threw herself against him. "Me and Rosita are making tea cakes. See?" She held up her hands. She was covered in flour and cookie dough.

"Michaela, what did I tell you?" Rosita bustled into the room. "You go and wash your hands right now."

Michaela pushed away and looked at him solemnly. "I got to wash my hands, Daddy. So I don't get your suit all dirty."

He nodded. "That's a good idea."

She ran out of the room.

"Too late, but a good idea." He chuckled as he pulled off his tie and unbuttoned his shirt. "Rosita, send these to be cleaned tomorrow, will you? I apologize for being late."

"Mr. Sean, you get into your room before you take off anything else. It is not proper for you to unclothe in front of a woman of my age."

Sean laughed and tossed his shirt and tie to her. "Right. Like you didn't powder my bottom when I was a baby." He headed toward the master bedroom, which was separated from Michaela's room by the kitchen and dining room area. At the door, he turned.

"I may be late for the next several days."

Rosita picked up his suit jacket and rolled it up with the shirt and tie. "No problem. My son and his wife have gone to Disney World. They ask me to go, but I told them all that walking was for young ones."

"What are you, Rosita, ninety?"

"I am sixty-three, you bad boy. I made you paella for dinner. As soon as the tea cakes come out of the oven, I'm leaving. Tonight is my favorite television night."

Sean showered quickly and pulled on an old pair of jeans and a T-shirt that said Miami Heat. When he came out, the apartment smelled of cookies. Michaela was waiting in the kitchen doorway. When she saw him her whole face lit up.

"Daddy! Try my cookie."

He swept her up into his arms and took a big bite of the strangely shaped cookie she held.

"Mmm. It's good." He kissed her sugary cheek and breathed deeply of her precious, bubblegum, little girl scent. "Who's Daddy's favorite sprout?"

"Me!" She pointed her thumb at herself.

"That's right. And don't you ever forget it!"

"Don't you ever forget." She shook her finger in his face, and he grabbed it and pretended to bite it off.

His eyes stung as she giggled and jerked her finger away.

*Don't you ever forget it.* He hugged her tightly and deliberately locked away the doubt his ex-wife had tried to plant in his head.

"Say good-night to Rosita."

"G'night, Rosita. Thank you for the tea cakes."

"Do you know what we're having for dinner tonight, sprout?"

"Hot dogs!"

He laughed as he headed for the kitchen. "Not quite. We're having paella."

"Pie. Eee." Michaela stretched her mouth this way and that, trying to say the word. "I don't like it."

"Sure you do." He set her in her chair and served up a small portion in a bowl. "Here you go. It's chicken and rice—sort of."

She picked up a tidbit of chicken with her fingers. "I like chicken."

"I know you do, sprout." Sean grinned and his daughter grinned back. "But use your spoon. You'll get more that way. Then when we're done, we'll get your bath and I'll read you a story."

He glanced at the kitchen clock. It was nearly eight. He needed to work out the details of the ransom drop. He never went into any situation without being fully prepared. But it would wait until Michaela went to sleep.

He didn't want to miss one second of the time he had to spend with her.

TWO DAYS LATER, everything was in place for the drop. Carlos had received a call from the kidnappers. As Sean had planned it, Carlos pretended to be too weak to talk, so Sean took the phone and identified himself as Carlos's personal bodyguard. He'd refused to meet them in an abandoned warehouse in a shady part of town and countered with an area in the middle of downtown Miami near police headquarters.

The man on the phone grew angry, but Sean hadn't lost his cool. He'd taunted them, saying they wouldn't dare try making the drop near Weddings Your Way. His bluff worked. The drop was scheduled for six o'clock in the evening on the far side of Weddings Your Way's large cul-de-sac.

Sean checked his watch. It was five-fifteen. He was in Rachel Brennan's office, along with Sophie, Montoya and a petite blonde who hadn't sat down since she'd entered the room. She was standing by the window, looking out over the grounds of Weddings Your Way.

Rachel Brennan was pacing. "We're ready, Rafe?" she asked.

Montoya's dark brown eyes snapped. "Absolutely. There is ample visibility on all sides. I have three video cameras set up. We *will* get everything on tape."

"But your men know not to approach, right?" Sean asked, repositioning the worn baseball cap that was sitting on his knee. He was restless. He wanted to be outside, in place, in case the kidnappers came early.

"But of course. My men are experienced in surveillance. There will be no mistakes."

Sean heard the words Montoya had bitten off. *This time.* It was a dig at Craig Johnson and by association, Sean.

His fingers tightened on the baseball cap but he forced himself to keep quiet. He'd wanted to use his own security team, but Montoya had argued that if the kidnappers were watching the place, they'd know all the regulars. A host of new people would spook them. So there wasn't a single member of Botero's security team here except for Sean himself.

Montoya's distaste at having to work with him was obvious. Sean could appreciate that the other man was as angry and frustrated as he was that Sonya had been kidnapped right in front of Weddings Your Way. But the important thing was to get Sonya back.

Now wasn't the time to get into a turf war.

"Sophie," Rachel went on. "You understand that you have to be completely in control at all times. You're going to be walking across that cul-de-sac alone."

As Sophie nodded, Sean studied Rachel. Her appearance fit with her wedding planning business—all feminine and cool and carefree. But her attitude didn't. She exuded an air of authority that seemed more suited to a law enforcement organization.

Sensing a movement from his right, Sean glanced at Sophie. His gaze followed her hand as it slid down her thigh, smoothing the material of her gray pin-striped skirt. Her reaction to stress. She was in her usual uniform—pencil-thin skirt that stopped just above her knees; soft, expensive long-sleeved blouse; and those sheer black stockings. Today she wore black sling-back pumps. She couldn't have been more inappropriately dressed for navigating uneven pavement carrying a suitcase full of money.

"Sean?"

He realized he was staring at Sophie's legs. He dragged his gaze away and acknowledged Rachel.

"I was asking if you had any last-minute changes."

He shook his head. "Not unless you can convince Ms. Brooks to wear something more appropriate."

Sophie's blue eyes glinted. "I don't see anything wrong—"

Rachel waved a hand. "If you can pry Sophie out of that tight skirt and those panty hose, be my guest."

Rafe Montoya burst out laughing. Isabelle, the petite blonde, joined him.

Sophie's face turned a bright becoming pink, and Sean was surprised to feel a grin soften his own features.

"I could give it a try," he said with a sidelong glance at Sophie, whose eyelids fluttered as her cheeks flamed brighter. She smoothed her skirt again.

"Oh, please. Get a room," Rachel said, chuckling.

It was a much-needed break in the tension.

Sean stood, wiping the grin off his face. "Let's take our places. We have about a half hour, and if they come early, I want to be ready." He headed for the door.

Sophie put her hands to her burning cheeks. Rachel's

offhand remark to Sean Majors had come way too close to the dream she'd had the past two nights that she couldn't seem to shake. A dream in which he'd done exactly what Rachel had said. He'd managed to rid her of her skirt, make a mess of her blouse, and run his hands up the silk-clad length of her thigh.

She'd woken up shocked and uncomfortably aware of her body's unfulfilled needs. She never had those kinds of dreams. *Ever.*

As she followed him down the marble staircase into the main salon ahead of her, she took the opportunity to study him. What was so different about this man that he showed up in her dreams?

Then, when he'd appeared this morning, driving a truck containing the logo of Weddings Your Way's landscape service, and dressed as a hired gardener, Sophie had found herself facing another, equally intriguing side of him.

Gone was the impeccably dressed young executive. His faded green T-shirt with the ripped-out sleeves exposed tanned, well-muscled biceps and emphasized his broad shoulders. A pair of ancient jeans molded his lean hips and powerful thighs. The jeans had to be ten years old or more. No designer on Earth made prefaded jeans that fit like that. As he reached the bottom of the stairs, he donned the frayed baseball cap.

Isabelle, walking beside her, nudged her, then nodded at Sean's jeans-clad butt. Sophie's face heated up again. She sent Isabelle a stiff smile.

Still, she couldn't deny Isabelle's message. Her

coworker was right. Botero's chief of security was sexy as hell.

She'd already acknowledged to herself that he was extraordinarily handsome. But today he looked earthy and supremely male, nothing like the sophisticated executive who'd grilled her about everything she'd seen on the day of the kidnapping.

This man, with his hair curling slightly around the edge of his cap and his strong neck and excellent body, exuded danger—the kind of danger that had gotten Sophie in trouble years ago. The kind of danger she'd avoided ever since she was seventeen.

At the bottom of the stairs, he stopped and waited for her. His face was solemn, his jaw tight, but she didn't miss the flicker of his eyelids as he checked out her skirt and her legs.

"You sure you can walk in those things?"

She stopped one step from the bottom. In her three-inch heels, she was almost six feet tall, and standing on the step above him, she was able to look down on the six-foot-two security chief.

"Pretty sure," she said primly. "I've been doing it for years."

His eyes were back to clear teal blue today, reflecting the faded green of his T-shirt. He took a step backward. "I'll be trimming the shrubbery on the west side of the house. I won't notice anything until you start across the cul-de-sac. Then I'll look up. It would be too obvious if I ignored—" he stopped for an instant, then gestured toward her "—all that."

She lowered her gaze and suppressed a smile as

she stepped off the stairs, her heels clicking on the marble floor. She wasn't unmoved by his obvious admiration of her figure. She wouldn't be human if it didn't please her that a man as handsome as he was found her attractive.

Rafe headed out the back door, through the pool area, to check on the video-surveillance setup. Isabelle followed Rafe, and Rachel had remained upstairs. She would watch from the third floor.

"You know where Montoya has positioned the long-range rifles. They will be trained on the pickup men. They obviously can't be too close, because of the width of the cul-de-sac. There's nowhere to hide."

She nodded. "Two are in the next house down, and one is on the roof of Weddings Your Way."

Sean touched her arm. "Don't worry. We've got you covered."

The brush of his hand against the sleeve of her blouse was reassuring. She looked down. "Your finger-nails."

He frowned at her and glanced down at his hand.

"They're not dirty." She touched one square-cut nail.

"Trust me, they won't be looking at me." He smiled at her and her heart fluttered. "Now I'm going outside and getting to work. I need to be sweaty and totally focused on my job when they get here."

Sophie swallowed and nodded.

"Remember, don't exit the building until two minutes after six. Even though they specified six o'clock, I doubt they'll approach until they see you. Just walk straight across the cul-de-sac, set the plastic bag down under the sign, and turn and walk back. Don't look back. Don't react to the sound of the car. Just walk, don't run, back to the building and get inside. Got it?"

She took a long breath. "Got it."

Sean went out the back door, leaving Sophie alone in the cavernous, elegant main salon of Weddings Your Way. She stepped over to the front doors, beside the bag that contained the ridiculous sum of money the kidnappers had demanded.

Checking her watch, she saw that she had seven minutes until she could open the double doors and walk out. It was going to be a very long seven minutes.

SEAN SNAPPED viciously at the shrubs with the pruning shears, not cutting anything, but working up a sweat. With dark sunglasses and his baseball cap, it should be easy to observe the action without being obvious about it. He hacked at the greenery a few more times, then lifted his cap and wiped his brow with his forearm. Not hard to work up a sweat in Miami in July.

He checked his watch. Two minutes after six. Where was Sophie? He put his cap back on and pushed his sunglasses up onto his forehead. The hot Miami sun gave everything a bright, overexposed look. The three immense houses visible on the street reflected the sunlight like polished metal. The street itself shimmered in the hot still air. With a flip of his head he dropped the shades back down onto his nose and squinted up the road beyond the cul-de-sac sign. Nothing. Not even a garbage truck.

He wasn't surprised. He hadn't expected the pickup

men to show themselves before the drop was made. He was sure they were watching. He had that itchy back-of-the-neck feeling. They would probably wait until Sophie had set down the sack and gone back inside. They might even wait until dark.

He reached behind his back and patted his paddle holster. His T-shirt barely hid it, but it had to do. He wasn't about to let her walk out there without his personal protection. He'd allowed her to become embroiled in this and he wasn't going to breathe easily until she was safe.

He heard the faint rhythmic clicking that signaled Sophie's high heels on the marble terrace at the front entrance.

She walked across the terrace and stepped off the curb onto the paved driveway. She moved slowly and deliberately, her head held high, her fingers wrapped securely around the bag. He knew it was heavy, about forty pounds. But she seemed to manage it without too much of a problem.

Sean used the tail of his T-shirt to wipe sweat off his cheeks and neck, never taking his eyes off her sleek, perfect figure. From her silky blond hair to her even features, to that dynamite figure and those incredible legs, she looked to him like the perfect woman.

If he were interested, she'd be just his type. Of course, he wasn't. *Not at all.* He had Michaela, plus a more than full-time job. He didn't have the time or the inclination to date.

Still, there was something about Sophie Brooks that appealed to him on a primal level. He enjoyed looking at the female form, especially one as sexy and sleek as hers. But it was more than just her looks that drew him. It was her attitude. Her demeanor.

Something about her resonated within him, like a tuning fork that picks up a perfect pitch and vibrates long after the sound should have faded.

A place deep inside him began to burn. It was a slow burn, a smoldering hunger he hadn't experienced in a long, long time.

He hefted the pruning shears and pretended to cut some more leaves as he surreptitiously watched Sophie nearing the sign. She glanced around.

"No, no, Sophie. Just set the bag down and come on back," he whispered.

She angled her head slightly, almost as if she'd heard him. Then she bent at the knees and set the bag carefully just under the sign.

As she rose, she looked sidelong up the road, then started back toward the Weddings Your Way building.

The faint sound of a car engine caused her steps to falter.

"Come on, Sophie. Get back inside. I don't want you hurt!"

Sophie heard the car gun its engine. *Don't look back,* Sean had warned her. But her CIA training and instincts told her to never leave her rear unguarded.

She retraced her steps back to Weddings Your Way, but the muscles of her back tensed as the car drew closer. Why hadn't they stopped at the sign to pick up the bag?

Suddenly, the engine's roar was too close. Sophie

glanced over her shoulder, her hand reaching for the holster at the small of her back—the holster that wasn't there. She was no longer a CIA agent.

The large black car was accelerating toward her. But just as soon as the realization hit her brain, the driver torqued the car sideways and skidded.

She heard a shout from the direction of the house and saw the glint of sunlight on metal.

She dove for the ground as a shot rang out. Her knees hit the pavement and she rolled, coming down hard on her shoulder as a second shot followed the first. Her elbow screamed with burning pain, but she kept rolling until she reached the edge of the pavement.

Sophie lifted her head just as something landed on her back. Something hard and hot.

# Chapter Three

The car spun, spitting gravel, as two shots popped.

A harsh voice boomed in Sophie's ear. "Stay down!"

She lay under the heavy weight of Sean's body, the sharp gravel biting into her cheek and palms. His chin rested against her hair and his left arm shielded her head. She tucked her face into the crook of his elbow.

The car's roar faded, its tires screeching as it rounded a corner. Sean's weight lifted for an instant, then he rolled off her. She sat up in time to see him reach behind his back and slide his weapon into his paddle holster.

He rose from a squat, his long, muscular thighs straining the faded denim of his jeans. As Sophie rose, Sean gestured at Rafe, who had rounded the building and was headed their way, his cell phone to his ear. He nodded in Sean's direction.

Apparently satisfied that Rafe's team was tailing the car, Sean turned his attention to Sophie. "Are you hurt? Did you get hit?" His face was smeared with dust, emphasizing the lines between his nose and the corners of his mouth.

She shook her head and took his outstretched hand.

"Sure?" His gaze surveyed her swiftly and competently. He touched the torn sleeve of her blouse, gently lifting the ripped flap of silk to examine her shoulder. Instinctively her hand brushed his away. "I'm fine. I banged my shoulder when I rolled."

He met her eyes. "Quick thinking, and an excellent move."

Sophie pulled her gaze away from his and looked down, avoiding the question he hadn't voiced. *Who taught you to move like that?*

Her silk gabardine skirt was ruined. Gravel had scraped the sheen off the fabric, and dirt and grass stains crisscrossed it like a finger painting.

She brushed at the material and winced. Turning her palms up, she saw the abraded skin. "Ow," she muttered.

Sean placed one hot hand at the curve of her hip and turned her palm up with the other, examining it as he guided her back toward the Weddings Your Way building.

"You're not totally okay, are you?"

Her knees and palms were scraped, her shoulder and elbow throbbed, and her heart was stuck at the back of her throat. She'd been hurt much worse; these were minor injuries. But no one knew that and after all this time, she doubted anyone ever would.

"Go inside and get someone to check you out. I'm going to talk to Montoya."

She looked back at the bag, still sitting under the sign. "What was that all about? They didn't stop."

Sean shook his head, his mouth grim. "I don't know. I'm not sure they ever intended to pick up the money."

"Wait." She reached for his arm. His skin was hot against her scraped palms. "What do you mean? Then why did they shoot at me?"

"I think this was a test. They agreed awfully easily to our choice of location."

"A test? To see if we called in the police?"

Sean shrugged as gravel crunched behind them. It was Rafe.

"Soph, you okay?"

She nodded as Rafe touched her shoulder in a protective gesture. Confidential's chief of security took his job seriously.

"I'm fine. What's happening?"

Rafe's black eyes appraised her quickly, then he faced Sean. "Go on inside, Sophie. Majors and I have a couple of things to straighten out."

BACK INSIDE, Sophie sat at the kitchen table on the second floor. She arched her shoulder. "I hit the ground on my right shoulder, and my palms and knees are scraped." She looked down and saw the shredded stockings. "Dammit." She tried to tug her skirt down, but it was too short.

Isabelle hurried in with the first-aid kit just as Rafe and Sean stepped into the room.

Rafe eyed Sophie but spoke to Isabelle. "She's okay?"

"I told you, Rafe, I'm fine," Sophie said.

"What'd you see?"

"I never saw the car until it was right on me. I tried

to follow Sean's instructions not to look back. I don't think the car had a license plate, but I can't be sure."

"There was no license plate," Sean said.

Rafe scowled as he dialed a number and listened. "Okay, guys. Good job. Bring in the videos. Let's see what we've got."

He put away his two-way radio. "Right. No plate, glass too dark to see through. You didn't get a look at the shooter, did you?"

Sophie shook her head. "Sorry. I saw the reflection of sunlight on metal and dove instinctively."

Isabelle dampened a square of gauze in alcohol and dabbed at Sophie's knee through her shredded stocking.

Sophie waved her away. "Don't," she said. "I'll run home and change. That will be the easiest thing."

She heard the muted desperation in her voice and hoped everyone would chalk it up to reaction to being shot at. She had to get out of these ruined clothes and stockings, and she didn't want anyone watching her.

She looked at her pin-striped skirt in regret. It was frayed at her hip where she'd hit the ground and damp from Sean Majors's sweat. As she brushed her hand over the back of her skirt she felt Sean's eyes on her.

Sean was all gritty primal male, with his bare, sweat-streaked arms, and a smudge of dirt on his cheek. His eyes were stormy as he looked her over.

"That was a pretty good duck and cover you managed out there."

Sophie stiffened. "Self-defense course," she muttered.

Isabelle quickly stood, gathering up the first-aid

paraphernalia. "Come on, Sophie. Let's go into the dressing room and I'll take care of those scratches and scrapes.

Sophie shook her head. "Nope. I'm going home." She reached for her purse, and winced at her scraped palms. For some strange reason, she began to shiver. "I'm—I'm fine. I just need a shower and a change of clothes."

"I'll drive you," Sean said.

Sophie stared up at him in surprise. She'd have bet he wouldn't have left the scene until he'd gone over every square inch of it.

"After all, it was my fault you were out there getting shot at."

"That's for damn sure," Rafe muttered.

Sean stiffened. "At least it was a plan."

Sophie rushed to defuse the animosity between the two. "All right, please. Drive me to my apartment. I'll change and we can come back here to discuss our next move."

Rafe caught her eye and shook his head slightly. She needed to watch what she said.

Sure enough, Sean picked up on the remark. "Our next move?"

She stood and nodded. "Sure. *Your* next move."

"Montoya, how long before I can see those tapes, and interview your men? Mr. Botero is going to want to know exactly what happened."

"Any time you want. While you're chauffeuring Sophie, I'll take a look at them."

Surprised at how shaky she still felt, Sophie directed Sean to her car, a late-model BMW convertible.

He stopped. "Maybe we should go in the pickup. I'm liable to get your car dirty."

She looked him over, moistening her lips as her gaze lingered on his dust-streaked hair, the T-shirt that hung loose over his jeans, the mud-caked work boots.

Then she looked down at herself. "I'm as covered with dirt and dust as you are."

"Okay." He reached to open the passenger door for her and the muscles in his arm rippled. She knew how good that arm had felt, curved protectively around her head. No one had ever put themselves in harm's way for her. Never. It was a new feeling. A warm and disturbing feeling.

Her body gave a little shudder as she moved in front of him and stepped into the car. Her tight skirt rode up, drawing a glance and a scowl from Sean before he slammed the door and walked around to the driver's side. He dug a cell phone out of his pocket before he climbed in and buckled his seat belt.

As he pulled away, avoiding the section of the driveway where the kidnappers' car had spun around, reaction to her near miss clutched at Sophie.

Her job with the CIA had been as a graphics expert. She'd spent most of her time forging documents, identifying and duplicating inks and dyes used in watermarks and aging paper. She'd never had any field experience, although she'd gone through all the training and kept her firearms proficiency up to date.

She sat stiffly, her knees together, her hands clasped in her lap, their palms stinging. Her body shook. She pressed back into the seat.

"So, did nearly getting shot turn you on?"

Sean's gruff voice held open hostility. He really didn't like her. But then, she'd gone out of her way to make sure he thought she just wanted some thrills. And better he think that than know the truth. She was bound by her loyalty to Rachel and Miami Confidential not to reveal her true interest in the ransom drop.

"Not as much as—" *Not as much as your hot body lying on top of me.* She cleared her throat and forced herself to remember that she was playing a part. "As I'd hoped it would."

"I didn't think so."

She gave a little laugh. "Maybe if I hadn't ruined my new skirt and blouse."

He kept his eyes on the road, his clenched jaw and his silence telegraphing his disapproval of her.

"You don't like me very much, do you?" she asked, watching him. He was so different today than he had been the last time she'd seen him. Then he'd been all business, the epitome of the young, stylish executive.

Today, dressed like a yard man, he was even sexier than she'd believed a man could be. The custom-fitted suit had hinted at a good body, but—Sophie moistened her lips and cursed herself for her weakness. She couldn't take her eyes off him. He was muscular and lean, and his thighs, wrapped in the faded denim, were awesome.

His eyelashes were light brown and ridiculously long. She'd already noticed the unique color of his eyes. His mouth was slightly crooked, which made his smile look as mischievous as a boy's.

Just the kind of guy she never wanted to get involved with again.

"I really don't have much of an opinion of you at all," he said, pressing a button on his cell phone.

That was a lie. Just the fact that he was working so hard to sound unconcerned told her that. And oddly, even though she'd never admit it, it thrilled her that he was affected by her.

"Javier, let me speak to Carlos."

Sophie pretended to look out the window as she listened to his conversation.

"No, don't wake him. Just tell him I called." He paused. "Nope. Nothing. Yeah, it's going to be hard on him. Stay with him. If you think it would be better, I'll drive over before I go home tonight and tell him in person. Thanks."

He disconnected and dropped the phone into his lap. Sophie had to use a lot of strength not to look at it.

"Sonya's father?" Sophie asked. "How's he doing?"

Sean's hands tightened on the wheel. "Not well. He's sharp. His mind hasn't been affected by the strokes, but his body…" He shook his head. "That's another story. I don't know if he'll survive if Sonya isn't found."

"We'll find her."

Sean sent her a curious glance, and she realized what she'd said. She covered quickly. "I know how good Rafe is, and today you risked your life for mine."

She shrugged and glanced at him sidelong. "Why would you do any less for your boss's daughter?"

AT HER APARTMENT, Sophie had no choice but to invite Sean in while she changed. As she turned the key, she tried to remember if there was anything incriminating lying around. She'd brought copies of all the police files home with her to study, but they were in her bedroom on her bedside table.

Her framed CIA badge and certificate were in the bottom of her underwear drawer. Thank God she'd had sense enough to hide it from casual visitors' eyes. Not that she actually *had* visitors, casual or otherwise.

"I'll be out in a few minutes. Please make yourself at home. There's water and juice in the refrigerator."

"I'm fine."

He didn't look fine. He looked irritated and impatient. She wondered why he'd offered to drive her.

"I should have driven myself. There was no need for you to put yourself out."

"Stop apologizing and get cleaned up. We need to look at your knees. I assume you have a first-aid kit."

"And first-aid training," she shot back. "I can apply antibiotic ointment and manipulate a bandage. I'll be out in a few minutes."

Sean watched Sophie walk away. Her skirt was twisted, the rip in her sleeve gaped, and a couple of blades of grass clung to the messy strands of her hair where it had nearly escaped its barrette. He couldn't believe how lovely she was.

He took off his cap and ran his forearm across his forehead, then folded the cap lengthwise along the brim and stuck it in his back pocket. He heard the shower start as he headed to her kitchen for a bottle of water.

The ringing of his cell phone jerked his mind away from an unwanted vision of her standing naked under the hot spray. A glance told him the caller was Carlos. He compressed his lips, then blew out a breath. Damn, he hated to tell him there was no news about his daughter.

He answered. "Mr. Botero."

"Sean, Javier told me you called."

The old man's slow speech told Sean that Javier had sedated him.

"What has happened? Did the kidnappers pick up the money?"

"No, sir. It appears that something spooked them. They drove up to the scheduled drop point in an unidentifiable Town Car and fired two gunshots at the woman who left the suitcase."

"*¡Dios mío! ¿Está viva?* Was she hurt?"

"No, just a few scratches. She was shaken up. It was an employee of Weddings Your Way." Sean paced.

"No news of my Sonya?"

"No, sir. I'm sorry."

"Sonya, *mi corazón. ¡Tráemela!*"

Sean heard the deep sadness and grief in the old man's voice. "We're doing everything we can to find her, sir. But the shots they fired were a warning. The car was much too close to Sophie for them to miss her if they'd wanted to kill her."

His body still carried the imprint of her trembling form beneath him as he'd tried to shield her. He'd expected to feel a bullet biting into his back at any second, but all that hit him was gravel as the car had peeled away.

The length of the living room wasn't enough for his long strides. He stalked down the hall and into Sophie's bedroom. "Mr. Botero, try not to worry. The money has been placed in Weddings Your Way's safe, and we'll hear from them again soon."

A manila folder lying on Sophie's bedside table caught his eye. He glanced back at the bathroom door, then walked over and flipped the folder open. It was the police file on Sonya Botero.

"I'd like to let the police know what happened."

"*¡No llames a la policía!* The kidnappers will kill my daughter." Carlos began to cough, and Javier took the phone. He told Sean he was going to give Carlos a sedative.

Sean thanked Javier, feeling helpless in the face of his employer's grief. He pocketed his phone, then rifled through a few pages of reports. They were copies of the same information she'd given him.

He frowned. Why would an employee of Weddings Your Way be interested in police reports as bedtime reading? That was going pretty far beyond the line of duty for a designer of wedding invitations. Had she wanted to make sure she was knowledgeable about the case before working with him on the ransom drop?

*How conscientious of her.*

A change in the background noise told him she'd turned off the shower. He carefully closed the folder and backed out of her room, taking with him an impression of a snowy white coverlet with bright pink and yellow and pale green pillows.

He made it past the bathroom door before it opened with a puff of steam.

Sophie emerged, wrapped in a white terry-cloth robe

with her hair wet and combed back from her face. She clutched the collar of her robe with one hand and held a first-aid kit in the other.

She stared at him with those wide blue eyes that seemed even wider without makeup.

His gaze traveled down the length of the robe to her feet. They were bare and damp, the toenails painted bright pink. He felt himself grow hard against the confining denim of his jeans.

*Damn it.* He didn't have the time or the desire for a casual relationship—indeed, a relationship of any kind. Certainly not with this woman. Even though he'd been attracted to her from the moment he'd laid eyes on her long silk-clad legs in the lobby of Weddings Your Way.

But her remark about excitement and danger had turned him off emotionally. He clenched his teeth as his body quickly reminded him that, physically, she still affected him. But that was lust, plain and simple. And the fact that he'd let it influence him pissed him off.

He wasn't even interested in the prim-and-proper Miss Sophie Brooks. Her cool demeanor obviously hid a wild side that rivaled his ex-wife's.

Her remark about being turned on by danger had sounded exactly like something Cindy would say. Only Cindy had taken her excitement with a side order of drugs.

The thought of his ex-wife destroyed the spell of desire that had taken hold of him like a face full of cold water.

"I'll be dressed in a few minutes," Sophie said.

Sean looked up. "Good. We've wasted enough time here."

Sophie winced, and he felt a brief regret for his rude response. But it was too late. He'd said it. He couldn't take it back.

"Of course." She turned and walked stiffly down the hall. At the door to her room, she stopped. "Feel free to wash up." Then she disappeared through the door to her room, closing it firmly.

Hell, he might as well. She'd probably be another half-hour, if he were lucky. He went into the bathroom and shut the door. Steam still lingered in the air and a heady aroma of something sweet and soft filled his nostrils. His body stirred as he recognized the scent. She carried it on her skin. It had filled his head as he'd shielded her from the rifle shots with his face buried in her hair.

He picked up a damp towel to wipe the mirror and found himself bringing it to his nose. With a curse, he checked the movement and quickly swiped at the mirror, trying to wipe his brain clear of the image of Sophie rubbing that towel on her naked body in this room.

She wasn't worth his time. In fact, he'd about decided no woman was. Not right now. He had little enough of that precious commodity, and every second that wasn't devoted to his job belonged to his daughter.

Turning on the water in the sink, he dragged the sleeveless T-shirt over his head and splashed his grimy face, then quickly soaped and rinsed his upper torso.

Luckily, she had antibacterial hand soap on the sink, so he didn't have to end up smelling like her.

He dried off with the damp towel, then ran it over his hair, feeling a slightly mean satisfaction that her pristine white towel now carried a few streaks of his dust.

The impromptu bath made him feel much better. Unfortunately, he had to put on the same T-shirt again. But it wouldn't be for long. He checked his watch. Five minutes.

At least twenty-five to go before she was ready. He ground his fist into his palm in impatience as he returned to the living room and gulped down the rest of his bottle of water.

He started pacing again. He was in a hurry to get back to Weddings Your Way and learn what Rafe Montoya had unearthed in the videotapes. He wanted to be sure they had checked the ground for spent rifle cartridges, as well as any glass or auto paint chips from Rafe's men's return fire.

He'd acted on impulse when he'd offered to drive Sophie home, the result of seeing her standing out there in the middle of the turnaround, looking small and vulnerable as the car sped toward her and the rifle shot rang out.

*Hell and damnation.* His protective instinct had kicked in the instant he'd heard the shots. Then, to his utter shock, he'd watched her instinctive response to the sound of gunfire. She looked like a perfect lady, but she'd ducked and rolled like a pro.

And there was that folder on her nightstand. There was no logical reason why she'd have it. Was that part of the excitement? Like the people who voraciously read every true-crime novel or had police scanners to listen in on crimes in progress?

She certainly didn't seem like the sensationalist type. But then, his ex-wife hadn't seemed like a drug addict, either.

He glanced around Sophie's living room. How long had she lived here? His wedding had been four years ago. She'd mentioned that theirs was her first assignment for Weddings Your Way.

She hadn't collected many personal items in four years. The furniture looked as if it had come with the condo. Everything was too sterile—too black-and-white.

Suddenly he flashed on the image of her bedroom. The furniture was the same black lacquered ultramodern design as the living room, but she'd put a pure white spread on the bed and thrown brightly colored pillows across it like confetti.

And her toenails were pink.

He blinked, just as his cell phone rang. It was Montoya.

"Majors, I've run through the tapes. Not much to see, although I know you'll want to look at them yourself."

"That's right, I do. Look, this is taking longer than I'd hoped. It may be late before I get back over there. Did you check the drive for—"

"Of course," Montoya interrupted. "Found two spent cartridges and some flecks of paint. At least one round hit the car."

"What are you going to do with them?"

There was an infinitesimal pause. "I'll take care of getting them analyzed."

"And those tapes—"

"I'll have one of my men run them over to your place if you like."

Sean frowned. The gesture from the Weddings Your Way security chief was unexpected. Still, it would save Sean a lot of time.

"I'd appreciate it." He gave Montoya his address. He started to mention that he'd talked to Johnson, but decided not to. That could wait.

He disconnected and glanced at Sophie's closed bedroom door. Ten minutes.

He stepped over to a chrome media cabinet, angling his head to read the titles on display. The variety of items there surprised him. There were a number of DVDs. He ran his finger along the spines. *Oliver Twist, Daddy Long Legs, While You Were Sleeping, Phantom of the Opera, Sneakers.* Eclectic mix, to say the least.

Her books were mostly fiction—romantic suspense, he guessed, from the titles and covers, but there were a couple of hardbacks that for most people would be odd choices. *A Look Over My Shoulder: A Life in the Central Intelligence Agency, I Led Three Lives.*

*Espionage?* He started to pick up the CIA book, then he spotted a slender trade paperback titled *Recovering Your Life.* He reached for it instead.

"What are you doing?"

Sean froze at the sound of her voice. It held an odd note. Was it fear? Or irritation?

He shook his head. "Just glancing at your movie collection. You like a lot of different things."

He faced her and swallowed his surprise at her appearance.

She'd turned back into the sophisticated lady. Her hair was pulled back in a severe ponytail. She'd applied makeup, and she wore a white short-sleeved top and a slim black-and-white striped skirt.

"I suppose I do." Her blue eyes turned icy and she lifted her chin.

Sean almost dreaded looking any farther, but he couldn't stop himself. Yep, there were the black stockings and black high-heeled pumps. Underneath the black nylon he could see tiny beige rectangles—bandages.

He had to force himself to breathe. He'd have bet money that with her skinned knees, she'd have worn slacks or a longer skirt.

He should have known it would be a sucker's bet.

But those knees were so vulnerable. She could have died out there today, and she'd known it. The feel of her quaking body under his had left him no doubt of that, but she'd refused to give in to it.

Suddenly he saw her differently. His gaze shot back to her face. She didn't want people—didn't want him—looking at her, knowing about her. Why?

Ah, hell. Now he was the one wasting time—time he didn't have to waste.

He picked up the keys to her BMW, tossed them and caught them in one swift move. "Want me to drive?"

"Could you do me a favor first?"

He glanced at her suspiciously. "Sure. What?"

"Could you put this on my elbow? I ruined three trying to get one on straight." She held out a large strip bandage and gave him a little smile.

She'd surprised him again. For a minute there, he'd thought he'd seen something in her. Something that made her different from his ex-wife. But her flirtatious persona was back. Damn, she was hard to pin down.

"Anything to help a beautiful woman maintain her image of perfection," he drawled.

Her cheeks turned pink, but she handed him the bandage and turned her elbow toward him. Her perfect skin was marred by a gash that must have been made by a sharp piece of gravel.

"That looks bad. And your arm above it is scraped, too. Are you sure you only need one bandage?" He pushed her sleeve up. "Let me—"

"No!" She jerked away, her hand tugging the material back down over her arm.

Sean went still, his hand up, palm out. "I didn't mean to hurt—"

"Never mind. I—I'll get Isabelle to do it."

"Here. I won't even touch it. It won't take but one second for me to slap the bandage on." He peeled it out of its wrapper and held it up with his fingertips. "No hands."

She cocked her elbow so he could get to the gash, but her other hand remained protectively over her sleeve. He slid the bandage over the gash. As soon as the adhesive touched her skin, she backed away, pressing it down.

"Thank you." She gave him a cool nod, but he hadn't missed the quiver in her voice.

There was something else he hadn't missed. The perfect Ms. Sophie Brooks wasn't so perfect after all. She had a scar on her arm just below the curve of her shoulder.

A large scar—an old one.

# Chapter Four

The man who had nearly killed Sonya Botero's limousine driver before was ready to try again. He gathered his paraphernalia together and prepared the syringe. This time, it would be easier. Last time, there had been no IV. He'd had to jab the needle into Johnson's chest while he slept. He'd gotten about half the dose in, helped by the fact that Johnson had sat up in bed, driving the syringe even deeper. The limo driver had lapsed into a coma and everyone had been questioned.

The good news this time was that all it would take to get the drug into him was a few seconds to push the liquid into his IV port. In less time than it took to inject the drug, it would stop Johnson's heart.

The bad news was that the driver now had a guard. The man's problem was twofold now. He had to figure out a way to get up to the eighth floor, because this week he was scheduled to work in the emergency room. Then, he had to get past Johnson's guard.

But he was a smart man, and careful, very careful.

Craig Johnson, limousine driver and security agent for Carlos Botero, wouldn't see another Miami sunrise.

AS SEAN AND SOPHIE climbed into her BMW, he looked at his watch. There was no way he could get Sophie back to Weddings Your Way and get home in time to tuck Michaela in. This was the second night in a row he'd missed her bedtime.

She was changing daily and he was missing it.

He rubbed his stubbled jaw and sighed.

He'd just drop Sophie off and pick up the truck he'd driven this morning. Montoya's offer to send over the tapes would help. He'd stay home a little late tomorrow and have breakfast with his daughter.

"I'm truly sorry. I'm keeping you from something."

"No problem," he muttered absently as he reached for his cell phone. "I was hoping to go back to the hospital and talk to Johnson some more, but it's been kind of a busy day."

"You talked to him?"

The sudden switch from polite apology to sharp interest put him on guard. His finger hovered over the quick dial button to his home phone.

"Yeah, for a few minutes," he said noncommittally. "He was on his way to the lab for a test."

"So now he can have other visitors?"

Sean slid the phone into his jacket pocket and sent her a sidelong glance. "No."

"Oh." Her blue eyes narrowed.

"Why?"

"Well, he was involved in the kidnapping. My boss is interested in what he has to say."

"I'm sure she is. I'm determined to get to the bottom of all this. I want to know how he's involved, too. But I don't intend to have him talking to anyone else until I've questioned him thoroughly myself."

"You still have a guard posted?"

"You're awfully interested in Craig Johnson."

"Rachel is interested in him. He used us. That call he made to Ladera could be an important clue to where Sonya Botero is being held."

"I need to be sure that's what happened."

"Well, as Sonya's driver, he was certainly in the perfect position to report on her whereabouts at any point in time. How did he end up with that job?"

"That was my call," he said flatly.

She gave him a knowing look. "You thought you could trust him."

"Obviously I was wrong." And he still didn't know why. He was a good judge of character, always had been. The talent had served him well in the private security business.

His gaze dropped to the dashboard clock. He dug out his cell phone and pressed the quick dial button to his home phone. Sophie dropped her gaze to her palm, where she concentrated on smoothing an edge of a bandage.

When Rosita answered, he could hear Michaela in the background, crying.

"What's the matter?" he asked without preamble.

"Ah, Mr. Sean. *¡Ella se porta como una mocosa!*"

"Like a snot-nosed brat? Michaela? She's probably

just tired." It was one of Rosita's favorite expressions, but she usually used it for her grandchildren, not his daughter. "What happened?"

"Today was the day she made pictures to show you. Remember, she told you she would draw you the big scary monster? Now she doesn't want to go to bed. She is crying in the corner."

Guilt whirled through his gut. He'd made a promise to his baby girl, and forgotten it. "I'll be there as soon as I can. Did a courier deliver a package?"

"*Ah, sí.* The doorman accepted it. I have put it on the kitchen table."

"I'm sorry to keep you so late."

"*De nada.* But please, for the sanity of this old woman, hurry home."

He disconnected and pocketed his cell phone, realizing that Sophie had stopped trying to pretend she wasn't listening.

"Brat?" she repeated, a tiny frown growing between her delicately arched brows.

"My daughter."

Sophie almost gasped aloud. He had a child. She hadn't expected that. He was certainly a chameleon. She'd seen him as a devoted bridegroom, a sleek and sophisticated businessman, and today as a gritty, sweaty, sexy man. She'd felt just how thoroughly male he was when he'd lain on top of her.

Even with gravel biting into her flesh, even with gunshots flying over her head, she'd still noticed the hard, hot feel of him pressed against her, his thighs surrounding hers, his arms protecting her, his breath on her neck.

But a father? "I—I thought you were divorced." Why didn't his wife keep the baby?

"That's right."

His eyes might as well have flashed a teal blue sign—off limits. He wasn't going to talk about his daughter or his home life.

That was fine with her. Any fantasies she'd had about why he'd offered to drive her home or why he looked at her so intensely had already been washed away down the shower with the hot sweat and masculine scent he'd left on her body.

Then, as she'd sat alone in the steamy bathroom, nursing her injuries, as she had so many times in the past, she'd deliberately banished the last remaining dregs.

No connections, no involvement, equaled no pain. And that's how Sophie intended to keep it. Unfortunately, not feeling lonely was harder.

As she sat beside him, the sweat and dirt gone from his arms and face, with as sexy and good-looking a man as she'd ever met, the loneliness dug deeper into her heart.

She'd planned her life carefully. Structured it so that she had no regrets, or at least she didn't dwell on them. All the things she'd lost, all the things she was destined to miss, she rarely thought about anymore, except maybe deep in the night, when she would awaken, frightened by a noise or a dream.

"Look, Ms. Brooks," Sean said as he exited the freeway.

Sophie looked up. "You can call me Sophie."

He didn't. "I really need to do something before I take you back to Weddings Your Way. It shouldn't be more than a few minutes."

Her heart leapt into her throat and she clasped her hands so tightly her palms stung. "Oh, of course. No problem," she choked out.

*Please don't let it be his daughter.*

He made a couple of turns, then pulled into a high-rise apartment building. "I made a promise to my daughter, and I'm late. She's supposed to be in bed by now. I just need to see the picture she drew me and get her tucked in."

Sophie's fingers began to tremble. "Fine," she said shortly, earning her a suspicious glance.

She did her best to pull herself back into Confidential mode, to think and act like an agent, rather than a nervous, quivering girl, but her shoulder and elbow hurt and her knees stung and she felt anything but cool and professional. She'd been in danger before. She'd certainly felt fear. But this man had given her a taste of what it felt like to be shielded from harm for the first time in her life, and it had weakened her defenses.

Sean Majors had gotten under her skin. And now she was going to have to face his daughter. *Just a few minutes.* She sucked in courage with a long breath. She could handle anything for a few minutes.

Couldn't she?

"How—how old is she?" So much for effort at conversation. She heard the barely capped panic in her voice.

To her surprise, Sean smiled. His face changed. His

mouth turned up more on the left than the right, a boyish, slightly crooked smile that carried in it a touch of sadness. Sophie looked down at her hands.

"She's almost three," he said, pulling into a reserved parking place near a bank of elevators.

Inside Sophie's head, the numbers ticked off. She swallowed and tried desperately to stop the inevitable path of her thoughts.

She was twenty-nine. That meant her baby would have been twelve. Her hand twitched to rest on her flat tummy, but she bit her lip and stayed still. It had happened for the best.

*It had.* With her background, she'd have been a lousy mother anyway.

She swallowed and pulled in a long breath. "Should I just wait in the car?"

He stopped with his hand on the door handle, as if he were considering that possibility. Then he frowned and got out. "No."

He came around and opened her door for her. "We won't be long."

They were silent on the elevator ride. Sophie had the feeling he was as uncomfortable bringing her to his apartment as she was to be going there.

Just as the elevator doors opened, he shot her a withering, disapproving glance.

She flushed. It was the bimbo persona. He was embarrassed, worried even, about her meeting his little girl. She closed her eyes briefly. She was an ex-CIA agent, a Confidential agent. Her job was playing a part.

She could do this.

He unlocked the door and leaned in to hold it open for her. The first thing she saw was an array of toys and stuffed animals scattered around the living room. The room was large, and decorated in muted colors. A long leather sofa was the focal point of the room. She saw balcony doors behind the sofa, with a child-protective gate in front of them.

"Have a seat. I'll just—"

"Daddy, Daddy, Daddy!" a trembling little voice cried out, and suddenly a small blond whirlwind in pink-and-yellow pajamas flew out of nowhere.

Sophie lowered herself to the sofa and watched in fascination as Sean reached down and grabbed the child.

"Daddy, I drew you the monster and you didn't come and you didn't come, and Rosita made me take a bath. I don't like Rosita."

Sean kissed her pale, tear-streaked cheek and laid his hand protectively around the back of her neck as he swung her back and forth. "Yes you do, Michaela. You love Rosita."

A middle-aged Hispanic woman with an ample bosom appeared in the kitchen door. "Well, Rosita doesn't like driving home this late." Her black eyes snapped to Sophie.

Unsure of what to do, Sophie stood and tried to smile.

Rosita looked her over, apparently unimpressed with what she saw, and turned back to Sean with a glare.

A flutter of dread quickened Sophie's pulse.

"Michaela, I want you to meet Miss Sophie."

The dread climbed up into her throat, closing it. Or maybe it was the tears that pricked her eyelids. Michaela looked at her and Sophie saw immediately that the child's eyes were the same teal blue as her father's. She was beautiful. A perfect child.

"Miss Sopee."

"Sophie," Sean whispered, exaggerating the *F* sound.

"Miss So-Fee."

Everyone's eyes were on her. She took a step closer, blinking rapidly. "Hi, Michaela. You're so pretty."

Sean angled his head slightly toward Sophie as Michaela buried her nose in the hollow of his shoulder.

"Eww, Daddy, you're stinky."

Sean laughed. "You want me to go live in the pigpen?"

Michaela put a finger over her mouth and rolled her eyes, obviously giving the matter a lot of thought. Then she shook her head and yawned. "Come see my drawing. It's good and scary."

Sean glanced back at Sophie, then sent Rosita a pleading look.

"Rosita, this is Sophie Brooks. Ms. Brooks is involved in the case I'm working. Would you get her something to drink? I'll look at Michaela's drawing, then jump in the shower."

Rosita sent Sophie another suspicious glance. "Ten minutes, you bad boy. You owe me many days off."

"Yes I do, and as soon as this case is over I'll send you on a cruise. How's that?"

The woman beamed. "To Cancún?"

"Anywhere you want to go."

As Sean disappeared into the room to the west of the kitchen, Rosita turned her black eyes to Sophie.

"May I get you something?"

Sophie's mouth was dry, her eyes were threatening to fill with tears, and her limbs had started quivering again.

"Please," she managed. "A soft drink or iced tea? I apologize for the trouble."

"Pah." Rosita waved a hand. "It is no trouble. But I am *muy* surprised. He has never been late because of a woman."

The woman's words surprised her. "Oh, this is not—"

But Rosita had disappeared into the kitchen.

Sophie sank back down onto the sofa. The big ordeal was over. She'd met Sean Majors's child and managed to get through it without freezing up or breaking down.

She accepted a glass of iced tea from Rosita, who stood surveying the living room.

"I suppose I must pick up these toys," she grumbled. "And finish loading the dishwasher. I spent the whole evening trying to keep the *muchacha* from crying."

Sophie nodded. She didn't know what to say. Then, as Rosita began to bend over, picking up stuffed animals and balls, she set her tea down and stood.

"Rosita, why don't I pick up the toys, and you can finish in the kitchen."

The woman straightened with a groan and gave Sophie the once-over. "Are you planning to stay all night?"

"What? No!" Her face flamed. "Mr. Majors is taking

me back to Weddings Your Way. But he had to stop and see his daughter first." She met Rosita's gaze. "If he could have avoided it, he wouldn't have brought me up here at all."

Rosita raised her eyebrows and muttered something under her breath in Spanish as she whirled and went back to the kitchen, obviously believing Sophie wouldn't understand her.

But she did. She spoke fluent Spanish. After all, she'd grown up in a Puerto Rican household. Spanish had been beaten into her all her life.

Rosita had said, *¡Acertó!* It essentially meant, *You got that right!*

As soon as Sean came out of his room, freshly showered and shaved, Rosita propped her hands on her hips and pinned him with those black eyes.

"I have a good mind to take off a few days and go visit my sister."

"Rosita, I need you here. I'll make it up to you, I promise. But right now, one of my men is in the hospital, and Sonya Botero is still missing."

"*Ay-yay-yay,* I know, I know." She waved a hand in his direction and nodded toward the living room. "Who is this one, then?"

Sean frowned. "She works for Weddings Your Way. She was involved in an incident today and I offered to take her home to change."

"Ah." Rosita's black eyes snapped. "And it had to be a blond one, eh?"

"Rosita—"

"At least she's smarter than your ex-wife."

He raised his eyebrows. "What makes you say that?"

She angled her head toward the sofa where Sophie sat. "She knows you." His housekeeper and former nanny nodded and propped her fists on her hips again.

For an instant, Sean stared at her in shock, then stole a glance at Sophie, who was tracing a drop of condensation down the side of the iced-tea glass she held.

"I don't know what the hell you're talking about. We just met. She doesn't *know* me, any more than I know her."

"Well, it is much too late for an old woman like me to be driving alone through the city. I will stay. Michaela might need me." With an exaggerated sigh, Rosita headed toward Michaela's room.

Sean blew out a breath in annoyance. "You don't have to chaperone, Rosita. Sophie—Ms. Brooks—is leaving."

"You have just told me you need me. Besides, I need a new TV. I can use the overtime."

Sean laughed and shook his head. He loved the little woman who had helped raise him and who adored his daughter. "Rosita, I should have you arrested for extortion."

"Yes, then who would put up with your late hours and your slave wages?" Her eyes sparked as she slipped through Michaela's door. "I will see you in the morning."

He couldn't help a small chuckle. So much for who was boss in this house. He was relieved, though. With Rosita to watch Michaela, he could get an early start in the morning.

As he stepped into the living room, Sophie turned her blue eyes toward him.

He glared at her. While he was in the shower, it had hit him what a mistake he'd made. What had he been thinking, allowing her to come up to his apartment? They were in her car. He could have just sent her on. The truck he'd rented was still at Weddings Your Way, but his own car was in the garage downstairs.

Well, he'd fix that right now. "It occurred to me that you could have gone on. You're in your own car. Sorry to make you wait."

"Oh!" Her eyes widened. She hadn't thought of it, either. "You're right. I'll—go now. I apologize."

She stood, reaching for her purse, and knocked over the glass of tea which, luckily, was nearly empty.

Sean reached for the glass at the same time she did and came in contact with her hand. She was ice-cold and trembling.

He took her hand in his. "What's the matter with you?"

She moistened her lips as her cheeks pinkened. "It's nothing. I'm just a little shaky. It's late." She paused and pulled her hand away from his. "Thank you for driving me this afternoon."

"You haven't eaten." She was exhausted and hungry, and some of her barriers were down. She seemed more—human, approachable.

"I'll get something on the way home." She reached again for her purse, her hand shaking like a leaf in a storm.

"You can't drive like that," he said reluctantly. His brain tried to tick off all the reasons for not letting her stay in his apartment one minute longer. But she'd been through so much today, and she hadn't complained at all.

"I'm sure there's dinner waiting for me. I'll be glad to share."

"Oh no, I couldn't." Her gaze went past him toward Michaela's bedroom.

"Michaela's asleep. It would take a bomb to wake her, which is good, because any minute now you'll hear a sound like a freight train. That will be Rosita snoring."

He waited, but Sophie didn't smile. It occurred to him that she'd been extremely uncomfortable around his daughter. Frowning, he reminded himself it didn't matter.

As soon as they managed to get Sonya Botero back, he'd have no further reason to see Sophie. So if she wasn't into children, it was no skin off his nose.

Sophie's knuckles whitened around her purse and she swayed, barely enough to notice.

"Okay, that settles it. Get in here." He headed toward the kitchen. "Let's see what the lovely and oh-so-polite Rosita has left for us."

He heard a surprising sound. Turning, he realized it was Sophie laughing. Her laugh was light, unaffected, and made her eyes sparkle and her nose crinkle.

When he stared, she ducked her head. "I'm sorry. It's just—your description—" She smiled again and glanced up at him from under her eyelashes.

"Well, Rosita is more like a mother than a housekeeper. She was my nanny. She raised me."

Sophie heard the love behind his words, and her heart twisted. A tingling sensation crawled up her back as she thought of the woman rearing him, rearing his child.

She recognized it immediately. It was fear for the beautiful little girl he obviously loved so much.

"Was she—is she strict?" she asked.

"Rosita?" He opened the refrigerator and leaned over, cocking one jeans-clad hip, to look inside. "Nah. She talks big, but she was always a pushover."

Emotions swirled inside Sophie—heartache, guilt, longing, the memories of pain and, as always, the shroud of loneliness.

Sean's devastating good looks and strong presence filled up the room. He smelled fresh and warm, like a shower, and the jeans and white T-shirt he wore traced the enticing curve of his spine and fit perfectly over his backside. He'd shaved, and his hair was damp and curling slightly at his nape.

It wasn't just his physical presence, either. This room, the whole apartment, was filled with love. It was as if he'd left the competent, serious security chief of one of the most influential businessmen in Miami outside the door.

In here, he was a father who adored his child.

Sophie was in way over her head, and she wasn't sure how she'd gotten there. Sean's obvious love for his daughter and his genuine affection for the woman who had reared him frightened her like nothing ever had. She didn't know how to deal with that kind of emotion.

She needed to get out of here. She should have left already.

She never should have come.

She repressed the urge to glance behind her to gauge the distance to the front door.

"Okay," Sean said. "We've got leftover paella, cold cuts, a big salad, and I smell fresh bread."

She jumped. "I—salad will be fine. It's late."

He nodded. With an efficiency of movement that awed her, he set the salad and cold cuts on the kitchen table and grabbed plates and flatware. "Do you mind if I open a bottle of wine?"

She shrugged and sat across from him at the table. After a few bites of salad and freshly baked bread, and a couple of swallows of wine, Sophie began to feel immensely better.

She looked across at Sean—at Botero's chief of security, she corrected herself—and forced herself to think about the events of the day. She'd been so wrapped up in her own misery and conflicting emotions that she hadn't really thought through what had happened.

"Have you talked to Rafe?" she asked.

He took a big bite of bread and looked up at her as he chewed. "He sent me the surveillance videos they got. He said they weren't much help."

Sophie's mind replayed that frightening moment when the car had spun and she'd spotted the gun. "I'll have to look at it."

He reached a long arm across to the kitchen counter and retrieved a flat box. "Well, here it is."

"Oh, no. I'll just see it back at the shop. There's no need—"

He wrapped a slice of bread around some roast beef. "I've got to watch them tonight anyway. And Rosita has a TV with a built-in DVD/VCR there on the counter."

He made quick work of the packaging and took out the high-quality VHS tape. "He's got a note here. This is the only one that shows any action, he says. Damn it, I told him to send them all."

Rising, he turned on the TV that sat on the counter and slid the tape into it.

"Rafe is good at his job." Sophie took a drink of wine and nibbled a bit of bread as she waited for him to fast-forward through to where the action started.

He sniffed as he sat back down. "I can see that, but he's a little territorial."

She smiled. "I know. He's always complaining about having to protect all us women."

Sean cut her a look. "Rachel Brennan has a large security staff for a wedding-planning business."

Sophie took a drink of wine to give herself time to answer. Rachel had instructed each of the Confidential team on ways to explain any oddities, but right now, with Sean's teal blue eyes on her, she couldn't think of one of them.

"There you are. I told you not to look around."

She looked up and watched herself surreptitiously glancing up the drive as she set down the bag of cash. She bit back a retort. Her CIA training was too in-grained, as was her personal protective instinct. She never went anywhere without being aware of all sides.

He and she sat without talking as the rest of the incident played out.

On the screen, as Sophie started back toward the Weddings Your Way offices, the roar of an engine could be heard getting louder. The car's passenger side slid into view from the edge of the screen.

She threw herself down.

Then from the direction of the house, she saw a lean agile figure leap over a row of bushes and sprint toward her.

*Sean.* Risking his life to protect her.

A pop sounded. Sean dove on top of her and wrapped one arm around her head as he jerked his weapon from his holster with the other. Then a second pop knocked up a puff of dust just behind her head.

She gasped.

Sean paused the tape at the instant the dust rose. "Are you okay?"

"That shot was closer than I realized."

"More excitement than you'd hoped for?" he said dryly.

She shook her head, too shaken to even be irritated by his repeated references to her remarks about excitement and danger.

She frowned, gauging the angle of the bullet. "It almost hit your shoulder."

"It would have killed you if you hadn't rolled."

He sounded angry.

She met his gaze, her mouth dry, but his expression didn't match his voice. He looked bemused.

Then he broke eye contact and restarted the tape.

Immediately, three more rifle shots sounded in quick succession.

"Rafe's men," he muttered. "At least one shot hit the car. Did you hear it?"

Sophie nodded, leaning forward. The car spun again, and she saw a pair of arms holding the high-powered rifle that had shot at them.

With a squeal of tires, the car peeled off, spattering Sean with gravel.

Sophie watched the screen in fascination. She was sprawled on the ground with Sean's body pressed on top of her.

As she watched, he lifted his head and brushed her hair back from her face. He said something. She nodded, and he rose carefully to his haunches, glanced around quickly, then held out his hand to her.

Funny, she didn't even remember what he'd said, but watching herself, she grimaced.

Her face on the screen beamed with hero worship. Sean had protected her. He'd thrown himself between her and danger. Nothing like that had every happened to her before.

"Well," she said, her voice slightly shrill, "nothing much more than we already knew."

Sean froze the image of himself gently helping her up as she stared wide-eyed into his face. "Montoya said he'd have the shell casings analyzed, see if they can be traced."

"Right. We'll do that."

Sean glanced at her as he stuffed the last bite of bread in his mouth and chased it with wine.

"You handled yourself pretty well out there, for a wedding invitation designer."

She went still. "I used to live in New York. I took some courses."

"Damn good ones, I'd say." He studied her for a moment, then reached over and touched her temple with his thumb.

Her gut reaction was to flinch away, but for some odd reason she didn't.

"You've got a bruise on your temple, right here."

His thumb was warm and gentle against the tender skin. "I guess my duck and roll wasn't as good as it should have been."

"No. It was good."

After a few seconds, Sophie blinked to break the spell his blue eyes were casting over her.

"So did Rafe say anything else?" she said brightly, standing and picking up her dishes. "Did they find any rifle casings? Any tire tread to analyze?"

"Good questions."

She heard the curiosity and suspicion in his voice again. Sean Majors was not going to be fooled long by the flimsy cover of Weddings Your Way. He was too sharp. Too observant.

She had the feeling he wouldn't long be fooled by *her* flimsy cover, either, if she stayed around him. She needed to keep her distance.

As she put her bowl and glass into the sink, she sensed his warm body behind her. He reached around and placed his dishes on top of hers.

"What did you tell Rosita?" His voice in her ear was low and gruff. The words were ominous.

She stiffened and turned around, brushing his chest with her shoulder. "What? What do you mean?"

"About us. About why I brought you here?"

"About us?" She shook her head, bewildered by his question. "N-nothing."

He was so serious, so intense—and so close. She'd gotten herself into a situation she'd sworn she'd never be in again. She needed to get away.

Taking a step backward, she ran into the corner of the refrigerator and lost her balance.

His hands on her arms steadied her.

"I don't understand," she said desperately. "What do you think I did?" Then it dawned on her.

*The bimbo who got off on danger.*

She lifted her chin. "I did not tell her anything. In fact, I told her the only reason I was here was because you needed to see your daughter. That you'd have preferred not to have me in your apartment at all."

# Chapter Five

Sophie saw in Sean's face that she'd surprised him. His eyes changed, turned stormy. He let her go and ran his fingers down the sides of his mouth. "I'd have preferred not to have you here. You told her that."

"It's true."

Sean blinked. "Yes. It was." He heard himself say *was,* not *is*. She was right. He hadn't wanted to bring her into his private world, his haven, where he was the daddy and his daughter loved him and he loved her in a way he'd never dreamed was possible.

He wondered what she'd think if she knew she was the only woman other than Rosita who'd been in his apartment since his divorce.

"I have to go," Sophie said, sliding away from him.

A dangerous impulse made him reach out and touch her temple again. He hadn't noticed the bruise earlier in the day, but it was turning dark now.

When he touched her, she flinched, then froze.

"This is going to mar your pretty face."

Her wide blue eyes met his, and he saw suspicion, wariness and something else in them.

"Who are you, Sophie Brooks?" His thumb caressed the soft, discolored skin near her hairline, even while he cursed himself for acting on the instant attraction that had been growing since the moment he'd seen her long sleek legs and delicate features from across the wedding salon.

Then all day today, as much as he'd tried to fight it, she'd insinuated herself into his consciousness. Everything about her fascinated him. She was beautiful, intelligent, remarkably capable of taking care of herself. But she also had a false side—the sultry, danger-loving side that reminded him of his ex-wife. And he didn't like that.

She shook her head, a faint glint of alarm visible in her clear blue eyes. "I'm nobody. Nobody at all."

And that was the enigma of her. She was such a contradiction. She had to be hiding something.

God help him, he had to know what it was.

He slid his fingers down her creamy soft cheek to her chin and lifted it. "Now that's one thing I know is not true."

She lowered her gaze.

"I saw you reach for your weapon."

She went totally rigid. "What are you talking about?"

He urged her chin up. He wanted to look into her eyes, see her reaction to his words. "When you dove in the parking lot. You slapped your back, right where a paddle holster would be."

"You're wrong."

"I can show you on the tape."

"I have to go." Her voice was tinged with panic. She pushed away his fingers.

He caught her hand and turned her palm up, still not sure why he was torturing himself.

He did want her to leave. If she stayed any longer, he was afraid every inch of him, and everything in his apartment, would be branded by her. She interested him far too much.

He wanted his quiet haven back. His sanctuary, where it was just him and Michaela, and Rosita to take care of them.

"I'm sorry you were hurt."

She didn't move, didn't speak.

He turned her arm and looked at her elbow. "That gash looks nasty. Did you put antibiotic ointment on it?"

"Of course I did."

"Let me rebandage it for you."

"No. Please let me go." Her face contorted with fear. Real fear.

What had he done? "Sophie, what's wrong? What are you afraid of?"

She shook her head, and tears glistened in her eyes. He felt something inside him crack when a single tear slid down her cheek.

He bent his head and pressed his forehead against hers. "I need to know who you are, why you know how to carry a weapon, why you don't like to be touched."

She stood there as if his brow touching hers had rendered her incapable of moving. Then she shook her head slowly, a negation that was almost a caress against his forehead.

The innocent contact sent a spear of desire through him. A part of his brain protested the stupidity of acting on that desire. He ignored it.

"It doesn't matter."

"Sophie—"

Another tear fell, and he kissed it away, its salty taste stirring a flame inside him. None of this seemed real. He felt as if he were in a fairy tale, dreaming about unwrapping layers upon layers of protective shell from around a lovely imprisoned princess.

A tiny sound like a sob escaped her lips, so he kissed them, too, and the flame inside him ignited into a firestorm. Her soft lips trembled under his. His body reacted, and his arousal grew hard against her.

She gasped and put her hands against his chest.

Before she could push him away, he covered them with his and kissed her again, more deeply.

Her breath was short and sharp. The fine trembling returned to her limbs, and her cheeks were wet from her tears.

"I can't do this," she said brokenly, trying to extricate her hands from his grip.

He let her pull away. Then he lifted his head and gave her a small smile. "Too much danger?"

She wiped a finger under each eye and swallowed. "You could say that."

Then she broke down completely.

Surprised, Sean caught her and swung her up into his arms. She was tall but slender, and her body felt strong and supple and right against his chest.

He turned toward the sofa, then changed his mind and took her into his bedroom and laid her gently on the bed.

She curled up in a fetal position and covered her face and cried.

"What is it, Sophie? What's wrong?" His mind ran through a litany of reasons that would explain why she'd suddenly cracked here and now, and not during the peak of the danger or the inevitable reaction afterward. There weren't many possibilities, and most of them had to be related to him.

On an impulse he refused to examine, he kicked off his loafers and climbed into bed behind her. He rolled onto his side, fitting his body against hers but careful that his still hard arousal didn't touch her. Gingerly, he put an arm around her.

"Tell me," he said.

"It's nothing," she said brokenly, making a half-hearted attempt to rise.

He wrapped his fingers around her upper arm and gently turned her onto her back, then took her hands in his and pulled them away from her face.

She closed her eyes.

"Are you hurt more than you let on?"

She shook her head. "No, I'm fine. Just let me go, please. This is wrong. I have to go. I can't be here."

His gut twisted in irony. "Wrong? Ah. Are you married? A fugitive? A secret agent?" He smiled crookedly.

*A secret agent.* Sophie's body jerked involuntarily, and her eyes flew open. Her field of vision was filled with his harshly handsome face. That crooked smile bathed her in a warmth that she had never felt before. It was kind and teasing and gentle and, yes, protective.

With dread squeezing her heart like a giant fist, she reached up and wrapped her hand around his neck. It was the hardest thing she'd ever done, and yet it felt right.

He kissed her gently, barely touching her lips. She drew in a short surprised breath as longing flowed through her, centering with frightening speed into the deepest core of her being. She trembled.

He lifted his head, his gaze cautious.

She moistened her lips, still afraid, and dared to do what she'd wanted to do since she'd seen him this morning in his sleeveless T-shirt. She ran her hand down his shoulder and over his biceps. It was as strong and sleek under her fingers as she'd known it would be.

His smooth, hot skin jolted her out of her passion-filled haze. Memories flashed through her brain. Guilt and fear crowded out the passion.

And she hit the wall she inevitably hit. The reason she couldn't do this.

She'd have to undress. She'd often tried to imagine seducing a man so thoroughly he wouldn't bother removing her clothes to get to her, but even if she thought she could have that effect on a man, the idea had always seemed sleazy and impersonal.

Yet the alternative was unthinkable.

Sean kissed her again, more thoroughly, driving all

rational thought from her mind. She grasped at the sleeve of his T-shirt and to her shock, her body arched against him.

Molten, liquid desire flowed over her as his lips sought out the secret places that had never been loved. The places she suddenly realized were aching for his touch. The soft skin behind her ears, the underside of her jaw, the sensitive place just under her chin. Running the tip of his tongue along her lips, he urged them apart and took her mouth in a deep, probing kiss that left her breathless.

Then he turned away.

She lay still, waiting. Maybe he'd come to his senses. He didn't want her here. He was about to throw her out.

She moved to sit up.

"I'm just turning down the baby monitor," he said, turning back to her.

*Baby.*

She'd forgotten about Michaela. Her heart leapt into her throat. He had a baby. *A family.* "Oh, no. I can't do this—"

"Hey, it's okay. Rosita's with her. They'll sleep all night. We won't wake them."

But waking the little girl wasn't what worried Sophie. She was getting in too deep. The baby, the warm loving family, the normalcy.

And Sean.

"Still," she said. "I can't—I don't do this. I need to go."

"Shh." He ran his palm down her leg, down her calf

near her ankle. His hot strong hand sliding along the sleek material of her stockings stirred her desire again.

If she wasn't careful—

He growled softly, deeply.

—he'd make her forget—

"Sophie—damn, I love these stockings." His voice was ragged.

He curved his body over hers and lifted one leg, laying his cheek against her calf and tracing it up to the surprisingly sensitive skin behind her knee with his fingers. Then he tenderly kissed the bandage on her knee, and slipped his hand up under her skirt. "Most women think they're too hot—"

Sophie had no idea what he was talking about.

His breath caught when he encountered the elastic band at her thigh, and the bare skin beyond.

"—too hot to wear in the summertime."

"Sean—" she said desperately, her body arching in shock and pleasure as his fingers brushed her bare inner thigh.

He straightened and tugged off his T-shirt. The perfection of his body made her shiver. Then he unbuttoned and pushed down his jeans. He was naked, exposed, totally open to her. There was no doubt how much he wanted her. No question.

Sophie put her hand over her mouth, feeling trapped. She'd gone too far. How had she let this get so out of hand?

He reached for the top button on her blouse and she grabbed his wrist.

"Please, Sean—"

"Do you want me to stop?" he whispered, feathering her mouth and cheeks with kisses as his fingers easily worked the buttons.

She couldn't speak. All she could do was lie there and wait for the inevitable. The shock, the pity, then the shutdown.

He pushed her blouse aside and unfastened the front clasp on her bra, touching her breasts reverently, then tasting each one in turn.

"Oh, please—" Sophie gasped in astonishing pleasure. She couldn't think, couldn't reason. Her cloak of self-preservation had been dissolved by the wet, erotic sensation of his mouth on her breast. All that was left was his gentle presence and the feeling that she was the most precious thing he'd ever touched.

When he undid the clasp of her skirt, she stilled his hand again, a halfhearted gesture.

He gently lifted her hand and placed it on his taut belly, then kissed her nose and smiled at her. "You okay?"

To her surprise, she nodded.

His smile grew wider. "You look scared."

Her fingers curled against his skin. "I am, more than—"

A deep, searing kiss cut off the rest of her words. He never stopped kissing her as he pushed her skirt down and ran his hands over her stockinged legs again.

Then he sat up and lifted her to push the blouse down off her shoulders.

Hardly able to breathe for wanting him, her heart thudding with fearful anticipation, Sophie lowered her head and closed her eyes. She'd never gone this far before. Usually the undressing was the first order of business, and she'd never made it any farther.

But Sean's hands, his mouth, were mesmerizing. No man had ever given her so much and demanded nothing in return.

She took a deep breath and waited.

He slid the blouse down her arms and bent to kiss her shoulder.

She shuddered.

He froze.

She tried to reach for the discarded blouse, but he stopped her fumbling fingers.

He wrapped his hands around her arms and lifted her bodily, pulling her into his lap with her back to him. His arousal pulsed against her hip.

She bowed her shoulders and covered her face.

For a long time there was nothing but silence, broken by his harsh breathing and her quiet sobs.

Then she felt his hot hand on her back. He spread his fingers across her shoulder blade. Her skin tightened as she flinched.

"Don't," he whispered raggedly. "Please don't be afraid of me."

"I'm sorry," she whispered, reaching again for her blouse.

"You're sorry. For what?" Steel rang in his voice. Anger. Shock. "Who did this?"

His palm scraped across the little ridges of her scars

as he slid it slowly, gingerly, across her back and down to her waist.

"My foster mother was—strict," she said, her voice small.

He was stunned. "Strict." He spat it like an oath.

Sophie cringed. Here it came. The shutting down, the withdrawal.

"This isn't *strict*," he growled. "It's a crime!"

He gripped her shoulders in his hands and to her shock, she felt his lips against her shoulder blade, against one of the worst scars, where a belt buckle had drawn blood so many years ago.

"Lie down." His voice was tight, controlled. He urged her down onto her stomach.

"Oh, don't. Please." Terror rasped in her throat. "This shouldn't have happened. Please let me go."

"Hush," he demanded as he lifted himself over her and proceeded to kiss each and every scar while she cried.

Sean touched his lips to Sophie's ruined skin, over and over, not missing a single scar. As he'd noticed earlier, the scars were old. Years old. It had happened when she was a child.

No wonder she'd looked so stunned when she'd seen Michaela. No wonder she'd asked if Rosita was strict.

Anger boiled in his chest, almost crowding out the horror. Almost pushing away his desire. He doubled a fist and cursed, wanting to hit something. But Sophie was so fragile, so panicked right now.

He forced himself to calm down. The fierce protectiveness he'd felt for her this afternoon when she'd nearly been shot engulfed him as he worked his way down her spine to the curve of her bottom, where more faint ridges swelled.

Her chest heaved with sobs and she lay stiff and unyielding under his caresses. Slowly, he rolled the sexy black stockings down her legs, holding his breath.

*More scars.* On the backs of her thighs.

He cursed as he traced each one with the tips of his fingers. Most were hardly noticeable, faded with time. But taken altogether, they spoke of a legacy of pain and fear that he couldn't even imagine.

He slid back up, torturing himself as he slid against her thighs, her bottom. He gently turned her over. She pressed her palms against his chest and the bandages scratched his skin. She met his gaze warily, shame and trepidation shining in her eyes.

He tried to compose his face. He knew anger and horror were painted there, but he needed her to know none of it was directed at her.

"Who was this monster? Why didn't anyone stop her?"

"It was the way it was."

"No one has the right—"

"It doesn't matter."

But he knew it did.

Cradling her head in his arm, he bent and kissed her with as much tenderness as he could muster. Her face was wet with tears, but finally, he felt her eyelashes brush his cheek, and experienced a surge of triumph and desire when she began to kiss him back for the first time.

"You're beautiful," he whispered, sliding his hand

down between her legs, seeking to stir her excitement until it matched his.

"No," she gasped, as he touched her intimately. "No, I'm not."

Her body told him she was ready, but she still held back.

He delved deeper, spurred by his own desire, caressing her, establishing a rhythm, hoping he could make her believe he was telling the truth. She was lovely.

She'd been damaged, deeply damaged. He'd figured out hours ago that something awful had happened to her. As bad as her foster mother's abuse was, he was deathly afraid it hadn't been the worst thing she'd had to experience.

He nuzzled her breasts as he continued stroking and caressing. He pressed his arousal against her and rocked gently, torturing himself with stimulation he didn't need.

Then at last, her legs tightened and she gasped. He looked at her and saw a light in her eyes—the light of passion.

Slowly, carefully he lifted himself and slid into her, watching her face. She was tight, hot. And a shadow of fear still darkened her face.

As he gently sank deeper, her eyes widened and her lips parted. She clutched at his arms and thrust herself against him.

"Sean—"

"Shh. Just follow me." He slid back and forth, back and forth, gritting his teeth, enjoying the exquisite torture of holding back as much as watching her respond.

Her eyes fluttered shut and she made a little noise at the back of her throat.

"That's it, Sophie. Just a little more." A lump grew in his throat when she peered at him through heavy-lidded eyes and arched her neck and moaned.

No longer able to hold back, he plunged, praying it wasn't too soon, hoping he hadn't frightened her. But she clung to him and her body clenched around him, squeezing every last bit of fluid and strength away from him.

He rested his forehead on her shoulder and sighed as she slid her fingers through his hair.

She said something, too low for him to hear. After a few moments, he lifted his head. Her wide blue eyes watched him. Her mouth was soft and full, and for the first time, her body wasn't tight or stiff. It was supple, soft, and molded completely, delightfully, to his.

He kissed her on the nose and rolled onto his back, pulling her into the shelter of his arms.

SEAN SLAPPED AT the bedside table as the annoying chime of his cell phone grew louder.

It wasn't there.

He sat up and squinted at the clock. Five o'clock in the morning. Where the hell was his phone?

His jeans were on the floor. He grabbed them and fished the phone out of his pocket.

It was Kenner, the guard he'd placed to watch Craig Johnson.

"Mr. Majors." Kenner sounded frantic. Sean heard shouting in the background.

Alarm knocked the haze of sleep and relaxation right out of him. "What is it?"

"Sir, something's wrong with Johnson."

"What? Kenner!"

"I just went to the bathroom. Two minutes, I swear. The doctors are in there now. They're working on him."

Sean cursed. "Stay there. Don't let Johnson out of your sight. I'll be right there." He slammed the cell phone down on the bedside table and stood.

"What's wrong?"

He froze.

*Damn.* Sophie.

He stood and slid the jeans up over his butt and fastened them.

She was sitting up in his bed, her hand clutching the sheet over her breasts, her wheat-colored hair loose and soft around her face.

Her eyes glistened. With excitement? The anticipation of danger? His stomach turned as he recalled how Cindy had always licked her lips and begged for the gory details of any exciting incident.

"Nothing. Get up," he snapped. "I've got to go."

Sophie's eyes widened and her hand shook. The sheet slipped a bit, exposing the dark aureole of one nipple.

A flash of raw desire cut through him like lightning, but he clenched his jaw.

She'd distracted him from his job. He zipped the jeans and grabbed a short-sleeved pullover shirt from his closet. "I said get up."

"Something's happened to Craig Johnson."

She'd distracted him, and he regretted it, just like he'd known he would. He should have gone back to the hospital last night.

Sean leveled his gaze on her. "Get out of here before my daughter wakes up."

A deep shadow flickered in her eyes, but she blinked and turned away, reaching for her clothes.

Sean's gaze lingered on her scarred back for a second as compassion gnawed into his heart, but he deliberately turned away. He had no time. Johnson could be dying.

"I'm going to the hospital with you."

"Like hell you are. You get back to your little fancy wedding salon and stay the hell away from me." He grabbed his cell phone and his keys and headed for the bedroom door.

When he flung it open, Rosita was standing there. Her quick black eyes darted from his face to the room behind him and back.

"Don't even start, Rosita. I've got to go. Get her out of here."

As he pushed past her, he couldn't help but glance back at Sophie one more time. She looked small and stunned sitting in the middle of his bed—as if he'd hit her.

His heart twisted, but he clamped his jaw.

He didn't care if he'd hurt her feelings.

*He didn't care.* He couldn't afford to.

While he'd been indulging himself, someone had gotten to Johnson. He'd promised Craig he'd take care of him, and he'd let him down.

Sophie felt Rosita's eyes on her as she quickly dressed. Her face burned with mortification as she did her best to keep her back to the wall. She certainly didn't want Rosita seeing the telltale scars. Sean's housekeeper already thought little enough of her.

When she finally had everything on, including her stockings, she raised her gaze to Rosita's. The woman hadn't moved. She stood at the door like a sentry, her arms crossed across her bosom.

"I'm so sorry," she whispered. "I'm leaving. Please, don't think—"

Rosita waved a hand. "I do not know you. I have no thoughts about you." The hand curled into a fist and she pointed her finger at Sophie. "But you can hurt my Sean, and if you do, you will answer to me."

To her surprise and Rosita's, Sophie smiled shakily. "He is so lucky to have you," she said in Spanish.

Rosita's dark brows shot up.

Sophie slipped her feet into her pumps, then she edged past the housekeeper and into the living room to find her purse and keys sitting on the coffee table.

"I didn't mean to—" she started, but Rosita's face discouraged talk. She propped her fists on her hips.

Shaking, fearful that any minute Rosita's deceptive silence would explode into anger, Sophie stopped with her hand on the doorknob. "I know you love Michaela. Please be sweet to her. Protect her. And take care of him."

Sophie called Rachel's cell phone as she sped toward the hospital.

"Brennan." True to form, the unflappable head of the Confidential Agency answered after one ring. She must have been asleep, but there was no indication of it in her voice.

"Rachel, it's Sophie. Something has happened to Craig Johnson. There may have been another attempt on his life. I'm on my way to the hospital now."

"Specifics?"

"I don't know much." Her face burned. She pulled into the right-hand lane and took the exit that led to the hospital. "Sean Majors just got a call from the guard he stationed at Johnson's door."

"Majors called you?"

Sophie's fingers tightened around the steering wheel. She opened her mouth, but nothing came out.

"I see. I'll call Rafe and alert him. Then I'll speak with the hospital's chief medical director. How much does Majors know about Confidential?"

It was a fair question. An important question.

"Nothing." Sophie took a deep breath. "He's suspicious, though. He saw me reach for my weapon when I hit the ground yesterday."

"What did you tell him?"

"That I'd grown up in New York. He wasn't convinced."

"Sophie, just how involved are you with him?"

Sophie turned into the hospital's parking lot and bit her lower lip. "Not at all," she said, hearing the hesitancy in her voice. "He thinks I'm a bimbo who gets off on danger and excitement."

"And yet he knows you've carried a weapon."

Rachel's voice was tinged with faint disapproval. Sophie waited, holding her breath.

"Sophie, I know this probably isn't the time or place, but I feel I need to warn you about something."

"Yes?" Sophie pulled into a parking place in front of the main entrance of the hospital, her pulse drumming in her temple.

She'd built her whole life, such as it was, around Rachel's Confidential Agency. The other members of the team seemed to like her.

Rafe worried about her. Isabelle and Julia and the others *teased* her about how she dressed. No one had ever teased her before.

If she lost her job with Confidential, she didn't know what she'd do.

"I'm quite familiar with your background."

Sophie gasped. She'd expected a lecture about the dangers of personal involvement during a case. Rachel had never mentioned Sophie's personal life, not even when she interviewed her for the job. She'd been delighted with Sophie's background in the CIA.

"I also know that you haven't had a relationship since you came to Miami."

"You know—?" Sophie had a comic vision of Rachel sitting at a bank of monitors, watching each member of her team. "I don't understand what—"

"Sophie, I'm trying to give you some advice. Some—personal advice."

Sophie clamped her mouth and eyes shut and waited. For the second time in twenty-four hours she was being stripped bare. After years of hiding behind her sophisticated clothes and cool demeanor, she was suddenly raw and exposed. Without defenses.

"Sean Majors had a bad marriage. His wife did drugs. Still does. She's infamous around Miami for her dangerous stunts and wild antics. She abandoned her own child."

Each word cut deeper into Sophie's heart. No wonder Sean had looked at her with such disgust when she'd told him she loved the danger. She couldn't imagine how he'd look at her if he knew everything about her. One thing was certain—he'd never want her around his child, ever again.

"I think he's very bitter, very closed off. Lives only for his child. Be careful, Sophie. He's probably not— a good choice for you."

Sophie pushed a hand through her hair. Rachel sounded embarrassed. "Don't worry Rachel. I have no illusions."

Michaela's beautiful little face rose in her vision. And Sean's wide, crooked smile as he lifted his little girl and kissed her.

"None," she said firmly. "I'm here, at the hospital. I'd better see what's going on."

"Right." Rachel's voice turned crisp and professional. "Keep me informed."

"Rachel, thank you."

Dead air greeted her last remark. Rachel had disconnected.

Sophie forced herself to concentrate on her mission as she walked in through the front entrance of the hospital and took the main elevators to Johnson's floor.

But her brain couldn't block out Rachel's words. They echoed down the empty corridors.

*His wife did drugs. She abandoned her child.*

Suddenly Sophie's knees shook so badly she had to

put a hand out to the wall to steady herself. Why had she gone to Sean's apartment? Why hadn't she just driven away?

She closed her eyes and leaned her head back against the elevator wall. If she had, she'd have missed the most awful, most wonderful night of her life. She'd have never met Sean's precious child. She'd have never seen the beautiful smile he reserved just for his daughter. She'd have never known such a deep love existed.

Now she did. And she knew more, too. She knew how tender, how loving he was. How fierce and focused. How strong. How protective.

Rachel's voice echoed in her ears.

*Not a good choice.* She laughed shortly. She didn't need Rachel to tell her that Sean Majors was out of her league. She'd known that from the start.

A man like Sean would never be a good choice for her. He was a good man, a family man. He was surrounded by people who loved him. She couldn't be a part of that, and she certainly couldn't compete with it.

The elevator doors opened onto the fourth floor amid chaos.

Three young men with sleepy eyes, their white coats identifying them as medical students, straightened and got on the elevator as she exited. A woman rolled a portable EKG machine around the corner and called out for them to hold the door.

Sophie stepped from the elevator lobby into the hall, where several nurses were scurrying with charts and IV bags and packages of tubing.

A couple of patients stood at the doors to their rooms, holding on to IV poles or shuffling their bedroom slippers. A male nurse guided one old man back into his room and closed the door.

A nurse pushed a red crash cart into a corner beside the nurse's station and picked up a phone. Sophie heard her request for a replacement cart as, beyond the bustle, a familiar figure caught her eye.

It was Sean. He was walking toward the other end of the hall beside a bowed-shouldered physician. In front of them, an orderly pushed a gurney covered by a sheet. Sean rubbed the back of his neck and nodded solemnly as the doctor talked.

At the end of the hall, the orderly pressed the call button for the service elevators and turned the gurney toward the doors.

Sophie's fears were realized. There was no doubt— the sheet covered a body.

Craig Johnson was dead.

## *Chapter Six*

Sonya Botero's limo driver and bodyguard, whom everyone had suspected of faking a head injury to avoid questions, was dead.

A lump rose in Sophie's throat. He'd been so young, probably no more than twenty-five or so. As the orderly pushed the gurney onto the elevator, she turned her attention to Sean.

He ground one fist into the other palm as he watched the gurney being rolled into the elevator. Even from her vantage point at the other end of the hall, Sophie saw the tension in his shoulders, the hard muscle of his jaw. She could see his grief. She knew he blamed himself. And her.

After Sean and the doctor followed the gurney onto the elevators, Sophie turned her attention back to the people in the hall. The floor was clearing, now that the excitement was over. The patients went back to their beds. Personnel who had responded to the code were gathering up their equipment.

Sophie picked up a patient's chart that was lying on

the counter and cradled it against her chest, hiding her slim purse. She approached a doctor in blue scrubs with a surgical cap and a mask over his face who was standing beside the nurse's station.

"That was the young man in—?" She paused.

The doctor started. He hadn't heard her come up beside him. Barely glancing at her, he nodded and crossed his arms.

Sophie pretended to consult something on the chart. "Cardiac arrest?"

The doctor grunted and sidled away from her. He glanced toward the patient room where a housekeeping employee was mopping the floor.

The nurse who seemed to be in charge was inventorying the contents of the crash cart. An obviously shaken middle-aged man was standing beside her and talking to her.

Sophie stood quietly, contemplating the blank front of the chart she held.

"—on *my* watch. That poor kid. Majors will probably fire me for this."

The nurse clucked in sympathy. "These things happen. I can't tell you how many times a loved one will sit for hours, then when they finally go for coffee, the patient passes." She opened a drawer in the crash cart and counted the contents, then made a note. "That's life."

"No," the man said. "Not when you work for Carlos Botero. Not when Sean Majors is your boss. Mr. Majors ordered me to protect him. I was only gone for two minutes. Did you say he coded?"

"Right. I was at the other end of the hall, giving meds, and I heard the heart monitor go off. Cardiac arrest."

"But he was just a kid."

"He'd already had a shock to his system earlier in the week."

"Yeah. I heard somebody tried to stab him with a needle. That's when Mr. Majors assigned me to protect him."

"It happened before I was scheduled up here. I saw a note in his chart, but there were no specifics. He was classified as a VIP."

Sophie moved smoothly toward the nurse's station and slid the chart onto a small cart as she eavesdropped.

"VIP?"

"Very Important Patient. The specific chart information is locked up, available only to the staff physician and the chief nurse, not to us mere mortals, but I heard—" She stopped talking as she realized Sophie was standing there.

The guard turned toward her. "Help you, ma'am?"

Sophie flashed a smile. "I'm looking for my cousin. She was transferred to Orthopedics."

The nurse peered over her reading glasses at Sophie. "That's second floor. Visiting hours don't start until seven."

Sophie nodded eagerly. "I have to be at work by then, and she really wanted me to bring her some— gum." She indicated her purse.

"Second floor."

Sophie thanked her and headed back toward the

main elevator lobby. She punched the call button, then stood just behind the angle of the wall, straining to hear.

The guard and the nurse didn't speak until the elevator bell rang. Sophie stood quietly as the doors opened and closed.

"Okay." The nurse lowered her voice to a stage whisper. "I heard that someone tried to kill him with a whopping dose of potassium. That's why he lapsed into a coma."

"You think that's what happened this time?"

"Potassium can stop the heart like that." The nurse snapped her fingers.

The guard whistled.

"But who could have done it? You didn't see anybody? I swear I wasn't gone but two minutes."

"Hey, we're shorthanded on the midnight shift. I've got seventeen patients. Some of the doctors like to make their rounds before surgery and interrupt my five o'clock medication rounds. Of course they can never find a chart by themselves. I had a doctor this morning who asked me for a chart that was right in front of him. Housekeeping was late tonight, too. Usually they're through by 3:00 a.m."

"Housekeeping? Was it the guy who was mopping Johnson's room a few minutes ago?"

"Don't ask me. I don't keep up with Housekeeping."

The elevator bell rang and a woman dressed in white rolled a bright red crash cart out.

With a sigh, Sophie stepped into the elevator. Just as the doors slid shut, someone stopped them.

It was the doctor she'd tried to talk to. He entered the elevator and stood next to her.

Sophie watched the lighted numbers change, observing the unspoken elevator etiquette that required passengers to avoid eye contact. But the doctor folded his arms and watched her.

She felt his eyes on her. She dared a glance at him. His heavy black brows were knitted together in a frown. Was he going to ask her what she'd been doing on the fourth floor?

She swallowed and stared up at the lighted numbers, feeling his black gaze boring into her. He unnerved her. She didn't think most physicians walked around with their masks over their faces. She looked down at his folded arms, dark and hairy, then on to his shoes, which were encased in disposable blue shoe covers.

When she got off the elevator, he stepped off close behind her—too close. A woman passed in front of her and she stopped. He bumped into her from behind.

He grunted and pushed her aside roughly and nearly ran an older man down as he took off down a side hall.

Sophie righted herself.

"What's his hurry? Are you all right?"

Sophie nodded at the helpful man and took off after the doctor.

He was almost at the end of the hall, jogging. Visitors and employees got out of his way—he was a doctor in a hurry. Lives could be at stake.

At the end of the hall, he slapped a metal disk labeled Authorized Personnel Only and slipped through double automatic doors.

By the time Sophie reached the doors and put out her hand to press the disk, a large man dressed in green scrubs materialized beside her.

"This is a restricted area, ma'am."

"Oh! I didn't see you. I need to speak to that doctor."

He frowned at her. "What doctor?"

"Blue scrub suit. Mask. He just went through this door."

"Sorry. You can't go in there."

She looked through the small round windows set high in the double doors. All she could see were dim overhead lights. "What's back there?"

The man crossed his arms. "You want the information desk at the front entrance, where you came in. They can page your doctor."

"But I don't know his name. Didn't you see him?" Sophie stood on tiptoes, trying to see through the glass in the doors. "It's very important. I have to know where these doors lead."

The man touched her elbow. "I'd hate to have to call Security, ma'am."

"But—"

He lifted his chin and squeezed her elbow.

She jerked away. "Fine." She looked at his nametag. *"Jimmy."* She glared at him as if she were memorizing his face.

Jimmy wasn't intimidated.

Sophie gave up.

As she turned and walked back up the hall toward the front of the hospital, she mentally catalogued what she'd seen.

The masked doctor had been around five-feet-eight-inches tall, a shade shorter than she was. He was Hispanic, with close-set eyes and black hair that the surgical cap didn't quite cover. He had a sprinkling of gray at his temples. A small, jagged scar at the corner of one eyebrow made him look as if he'd been in a barroom brawl.

She remembered Samantha's description of the man who'd attacked her outside Johnson's room a couple of weeks ago. He'd been dressed in scrubs with a surgical mask over his face, just like this guy. But Samantha had insisted he wasn't a doctor. She'd said his fingernails were dirty.

Sophie looked down at her shoulder, where the man's dark hand had gripped her white blouse as he'd shoved her out of the way. There was a smear of black on her shoulder.

She could be wearing evidence of a killer.

THE MAN WALKED quickly through the emergency room doors and out into the parking lot. He'd ripped off the surgical cap and the mask and tugged off the scrub shirt, exposing his sleeveless undershirt. He sprinted around the side of the building and stood at the corner of the main entrance, pretending to fool with an empty cigarette pack he'd grabbed from the trash can where he'd stuffed the scrubs.

A couple of people walking by in the early light of sunrise gave him wary looks, but he just kept his head down, watching the entrance sidelong.

There she was. The tall blonde who'd chased him.

She burst through the front doors, glancing around. She was still looking for him.

He chuckled. Now that he'd accomplished his mission, he felt the giddy euphoria that always came with a job well done. It had taken him all night to get into the perfect position to take care of Botero's limo driver.

Luckily, he was a patient man, a careful man. He never hurried. It was what made him so good at his job.

As the woman propped her fists on her hips in obvious frustration, he studied her. He'd know her if he ever saw her again, and in a couple of minutes, he'd know her car.

She was a knockout, with those long legs and that pale hair. How was she involved with all this? More importantly, why had she followed him? What had she seen?

Was it because he'd watched her in the elevator? He shook his head. *No.* A woman like her—she'd just ignore him and get away as soon as possible. She'd seen something—figured out something.

She started across the parking lot.

He sidled closer to the front entrance, keeping her in his line of sight as she climbed into a BMW convertible. The maneuver revealed an incredible length of shapely thigh.

For an instant, he indulged himself in the thought of her spread-eagled, at his mercy, her cool blue eyes sunken and bright with fear. The thought made his mouth water and his groin stir and itch.

As she settled into the driver's seat, he hit a preset number on his cell phone and spoke in Spanish.

"It's Fuentes. Find out who this woman is. She

noticed me." He recited her license plate to the person on the other end of the line.

She pulled out of the parking lot, her gaze sweeping past him without seeing him, and drove away.

"No, I do not know. You have connections. Use them."

He glanced at his phone as he disconnected.

Damn. That was it. He'd dressed like a doctor, but he'd neglected one important point. He squeezed the phone in his fist as he looked at his hand.

"*¡Qué ingeniosa!* Smart girl."

He pocketed the phone and walked back around to the emergency room entrance. He still had about an hour before the end of his shift.

Then he'd wait to find out who she was and where she lived. It would be a pleasure to take care of her.

He'd show her what dirty fingernails could do.

AFTER A HOT SHOWER and a change of clothes, Sophie carefully placed her blouse in a paper bag and headed to Weddings Your Way. Unfortunately, she had an appointment with a bride at ten o'clock. And Rachel's first rule was that the Confidential team never expose their cover.

When she'd entered her apartment, she'd stopped cold. Her haven, her retreat from the world was different. Sean had been there. He'd touched her books, washed up in her bathroom, waited while she'd showered.

Then in her bedroom, she'd spotted the Botero case file on her bedside table. She knew immediately that Sean had touched it. The corner of one sheet of paper was askew, its edge adding a white border to the dull yellow of the manila folder.

She'd made too many mistakes in the past twenty-four hours. Broken so many of her personal rules. Sacrificed too much of her hard-won privacy.

And for what? A brief connection with another human being? A fleeting sense that someone cared more for her safety than for his own? A glimpse of a side of family life that would never be hers?

As she sped along the freeway in the bright heat and suffocating humidity, she had a mortifying thought. She glanced at the folder in the passenger seat and pictured Sean standing beside her bed, inspecting its contents.

Had he seduced her to get information? Shame blanketed her. If that had been his intent, he'd gone to a lot of trouble. He'd been in her apartment. Why bring her to his? Especially when she knew she was right about him. He hadn't wanted her invading his private life, meeting his daughter.

Could he really have been overcome by their closeness, as she was? For an instant she sank into memory of his powerful body covering hers, his gentle lips tracing each telltale scar on her back and legs.

"Stop it!" It didn't matter why he'd done it. It was over. He'd kicked her out.

She needed to concentrate on the case. She needed to let Rafe know about the man in the surgical mask. About the evidence on her blouse. She glanced at her dashboard clock, then dialed his cell phone.

"Montoya." His voice was hushed.

"Rafe, it's Sophie."

"You okay?"

"Yes, of course," she answered automatically. "I just need—"

"I'll call you back."

"But—"

"We're getting the autopsy report on Johnson. Are you at the office?"

"On my way."

Rafe disconnected.

Sophie sighed. The autopsy report was the most important thing. They'd soon have proof that Johnson was murdered. Her information could wait.

She changed lanes, preparing to exit. As she maneuvered the exit ramp, a dark car forced its way around her.

"What are you doing?" she shouted as she veered closer to the guardrail and braked. But the car kept coming.

Its fender scraped hers with a screech of metal.

Desperately, Sophie glanced in her rearview mirror. There was a line of cars behind her, and this madman beside her.

She braked again, afraid to take her eyes off the guardrail to look at the other car. Her right fender scraped the rail.

Horns were honking, tires were squealing, the dark car sped up and cut toward the right.

Gripping the wheel like a lifeline, Sophie braked, expecting to feel the impact of the cars behind her as the front car cut her off.

Suddenly, the dark car shot forward, off the ramp and onto the busy highway, nearly cutting off a new Lexus.

Sophie fought to maintain control of her car and

herself as she entered the merge lane and pulled forward until she could slow down and stop.

She sat there in the driver's seat, trembling violently. Tears streamed down her cheeks unchecked as the full impact of what had just happened slammed into her.

She covered her mouth with shaky fingers, trying to force herself to breathe normally.

A tap on her window caused her to jump and look up in surprise.

"Hey! Are you all right?"

It was a man dressed in a mechanic's uniform. A glance in her rearview mirror revealed a white pickup.

She nodded and lowered her window a fraction. "I'm—" Her voice cracked. "I'm fine."

"What a jerk," the mechanic went on, looking over his shoulder in the direction the car had gone. "I didn't get a license, but it was a late-model Ford. Tinted windows. We should call the police."

"No," Rachel said hurriedly. "Truly, I'm fine. They'll never find him." She smiled. "You know how it goes."

The man took a step backward and inspected her car. "You got a really bad scrape there." He reached in his pocket. "I work with a good body shop." He held out a card.

She took it without looking at it. "I don't suppose you saw the driver's face?"

The man shook his head. "Like I said. Tinted windows. Those things should be outlawed. You sure you're okay?"

Sophie assured him and thanked him for stopping to check on her.

She dialed Rafe again, but he didn't answer.

She started her car and pulled out into traffic, her hands still quivering, her stomach roiling.

"When did you get to be such a wimp?" she asked herself in disgust. She shouldn't have pulled over. She should have chased the car.

But she knew it wouldn't have done any good. He'd nearly wrecked a Lexus to get away from her. She'd never have caught up with him.

One thing she did know. The driver of the dark car had targeted her specifically. It was no accident. She glanced at the bag containing her blouse. Someone was worried about what she'd seen.

But how had they found her?

Suddenly, the truth hit her. She'd been followed from the hospital.

The killers knew where she lived.

SEAN SPENT the next couple of hours talking with the physician in charge about the specifics surrounding Craig Johnson's death. He called and broke the news to Craig's parents. Autopsies were automatically done in the event of a suspicious death, but Sean didn't tell them their son might have been murdered.

Then he spoke extensively with Kenner and interviewed the midnight-shift employees who were on duty when Johnson had coded.

Just as he was finishing up with the last of the employees who admitted being on the fourth floor during the night, Rachel Brennan and Rafe Montoya showed up with a hospital security officer. Rachel was talking on her cell phone.

Sean had placed Kenner at the door to Johnson's room to secure it. Montoya dismissed Kenner and directed the hospital's guard to lock the door.

He stalked over to confront Montoya, nodding at Kenner to back off.

"What's going on, Montoya?"

"Majors." Rafe, dressed in a jacket and tie, gave Sean's jeans and pullover shirt the once-over.

Behind him, Rachel snapped her phone shut. "Hello, Mr. Majors. I'm terribly sorry about Craig Johnson. Please offer my condolences to his family."

Sean frowned at her. He didn't buy her casual attitude or her easy sympathy. "I'm sure that will mean a lot to them," he said evenly, then turned his attention back to Rafe.

"I assume you're here because Sophie called you."

Montoya lifted his chin, his eyes glittering. "That's right, Majors. She called *us*. If I were you—"

"Mr. Majors." Rachel took a minuscule step forward. "Perhaps it would be best if you let us deal with the hospital officials."

"This is a *murder*, Ms. Brennan. Not a misplaced bridesmaid dress."

Montoya bristled, but Rachel held up a manicured finger. "In fact, we don't know yet that Mr. Johnson was murdered. I'd like to handle this with a minimum of publicity, so why don't we meet in the chief medical director's office in—" she glanced at her watch "—ten minutes?"

"Publicity," Sean spat. "Yeah. That's the most important thing."

Rachel's mouth tightened. "I feel sure you have no more desire than we do to stir up the media. I know Mr. Botero doesn't need the added stress."

Sean clamped his jaw. He couldn't quite dislike Rachel Brennan, but her extraordinary composure combined with an undeniable instinct for handling difficult situations made him suspicious.

This woman knew what she was doing, and she and her staff were more than what they seemed to be. It galled him that he couldn't figure her out.

Her or Sophie.

Without waiting for an answer, Rachel smiled at him and headed for the elevators. Montoya moved into step beside her, and the hospital guard followed meekly behind.

Sean stared at the locked hospital room, frustration and regret weighing heavily on his heart.

"Sort of makes it seem final, doesn't it?" Kenner spoke at his elbow, voicing his thoughts. "That Johnson was a nice kid. He had tons of stories from his tour in Iraq. Wonder how he got mixed up in all this."

Sean shook his head. He'd thought Craig was a nice kid, too. And he'd always prided himself on his judgment. How had he been fooled by Johnson?

He could only think of two reasons why anyone would risk coming into a hospital to kill someone. Either Johnson had seen something, or he'd been involved. Given his admission about gambling debts, Sean was certain it was the latter.

"I remember when he was hired. I couldn't believe he was old enough to be out of college." Kenner rubbed his chin. "When was that? Three years ago, wasn't it?"

Sean nodded. "In the fall." *Three years ago.* That was right after Michaela was born.

Unhappy memories blindsided him, throwing him back in time.

It should have been the best time of his life, but Cindy had been unhappy and jealous of the baby. It was only a couple of months later that she'd left Michaela and him.

Right about the time he'd hired Johnson. He cursed to himself. If he hadn't been distracted by Cindy's abandonment and the needs of his new daughter, would he have made a different decision?

"Sir?"

"Nothing, Kenner. Get back to Carlos's. I need you to sit down and write out every single thing you remember, no matter how small, no matter how insignificant."

"Mr. Majors, I feel responsible—"

"Don't. It's obvious that whoever did this was waiting for the perfect opportunity. It was going to happen sooner or later. If anything, it's my fault. I should have posted two guards."

Sean squeezed Kenner's shoulder. "You did a good job. Now give me your report. Your observations will help us find out what happened."

"Yes, sir." Kenner stood a little taller as he headed toward the elevators.

Sean glanced back at the locked hospital room and shook his head in regret.

"Oh, Mr. Majors." Kenner approached him again. "I meant to tell you. There was a woman lurking around here about the time you and the doctor were taking Johnson downstairs. At first, I thought she was a doctor. She was carrying a chart."

Sean waited.

"But she didn't have a coat or a name tag."

"Well, who was she? A visitor?"

Kenner looked thoughtful for a second, then shook his head. "No, sir. I don't think so. She was listening to us."

"To who?"

"The nurse and me. While everybody was cleaning up from the code, the night nurse was explaining to me about how a dose of potassium into an IV could stop the heart."

*Listening.* A dread certainty took hold of him. "What about the woman? What did she look like?"

Kenner smiled and shook his head. "I have to tell you, she was a knockout. Tall and blond, with legs—"

Sean blew out a frustrated breath. "How was she dressed?"

"Some kind of little skirt and top, with black stockings."

It was Sophie. It had to be. There couldn't be two blondes in Miami who would be dressed in black stockings at the crack of dawn. His brain surprised him with the remembered feel of those stockings against his palm, against his cheek. A shiver of longing coursed through him.

"How long was she here?"

"Can't say. But she was one of the last to leave. All the patients were back in their rooms and Housekeeping was mopping up Johnson's room. I asked her if she needed some help and she spouted some story about looking for her cousin."

"Thanks, Kenner. Make sure you put that in your report."

"Yes, sir."

As Kenner left, Sean gritted his teeth. Damn it. When he'd left her in his bed this morning, he'd told her to leave. He should have known she'd follow him here.

He didn't know who or what she was, but it was a cinch she wasn't just an invitation designer for an upscale wedding-planning salon.

She was too savvy. She'd played him until he'd agreed to let her make the ransom drop. Then she'd played him some more.

She'd tapped into too many of his secret places. His secret fantasy of long black-stockinged legs. His protective instinct. The compassion that rose so easily when he saw injustice or abuse.

And she'd done it all for one reason. To find out everything he knew. The question was, *why?*

He ground his fist into his palm. It didn't matter why. She was a distraction, and he had no room in his life for distractions. He had an obligation to Carlos Botero, and now to Craig Johnson.

He didn't want anything else to do with Sophie Brooks. He didn't want to think about her, didn't want to see her. He sure didn't want to feel anything for her. He needed all his focus, all his attention, to find Sonya's kidnappers and Johnson's murderer.

TWENTY MINUTES LATER, Sean sat in the richly appointed offices of the chief medical director of the hospital. He'd expected to see Rachel Brennan and Rafe Montoya there, but the presence of the police commissioner had surprised him.

The medical director assured him that the hospital was handling the autopsy and that as soon as they had a cause of death, he would be notified.

Sean shook his head and laughed. "Notified. That was one of my men who died in there. It's my case."

"I had occasion to speak with your employer this morning, Mr. Majors," the police commissioner said.

"You've talked with Mr. Botero?" Anger boiled up inside him. It took a huge effort to keep his voice calm. "He is very ill. I'm his chief of security, and I've worked extremely hard to keep him informed without upsetting him. Why didn't you go through me?"

"I assure you, there was no intent to go over your head, Mr. Majors, but I cannot overemphasize the sensitive nature of this matter."

Sean bristled. "I am aware of the sensitivity of *this matter.* I'm also aware of the seriousness. Someone murdered Craig Johnson, and my employer's daughter is still missing." He looked pointedly at the police commissioner. "Mr. Botero asked me personally not to involve the police."

He looked around the room. "Yet here we are. You

did go over my head. And now I find that a wedding planner and her rent-a-cop have more information about this case than I do." This time, he didn't try to keep the sarcasm out of his voice.

He saw Montoya's face grow dark with anger. He also saw Rachel Brennan's manicured hand move in an almost imperceptible gesture.

Montoya, who had grabbed the arms of his chair, consciously relaxed his hands.

"We need your cooperation, Mr. Majors," Rachel Brennan said.

Sean sent her an ironic glance. "Yes, you do. I need explanations, Ms. Brennan."

The police commissioner cleared his throat. "I'm afraid at this point, you must be content to trust us. There are some very touchy international matters that cannot be disturbed right now. We have no choice but to maintain a low profile."

Sean stood, his chair scraping the hardwood floor. "I am aware of the situation in Ladera, and of Juan DeLeon's involvement. I have no reason to interfere with any matter concerning them. But I will not maintain a low profile. I have a murderer and a kidnapper to catch. I can do this alone if I have to. You will find, though, that you would rather have me as a friend than as an enemy."

"Are you threatening me, Mr. Majors?" The commissioner scowled.

"Not at all. I'm merely informing you of *my* plan. I will continue my own investigation into the matters that concern Mr. Botero."

He stood there for a few seconds, as glances passed among the seated participants. Then, straightening his back, he turned on his heel and left.

In the hall, he slammed his palm against a door facing, the resulting pain making him feel slightly better. He reared back to do it again, but a student nurse passing by looked at him in alarm, so he doubled his fist at his side instead.

He stalked to his car and headed toward Botero's estate, dialing the cell phone of his second-in-command, Al Lopez.

"Lopez, everything all right there?"

"Fine. I heard about Johnson." Lopez didn't waste words or time. It was his biggest asset.

"Yeah. Kenner's pretty shaken up. He'll be turning in a report. Let me know when he gets it done, will you? And keep him busy. He's got the idea this was his fault."

"Was it?"

"No. I should have had two guards posted."

"Maybe."

Sean knew Lopez wasn't sure that two guards would have been any better able to protect Johnson than one. Neither was he. But he still felt responsible.

"I understand the police commissioner called Carlos. How'd he take it?"

"Not good. He thought the commissioner had word about Sonya. Javier said he almost collapsed."

"Damn it." Frustration burned in his gut. "I'm on my way over there. I want a meeting with the team."

"Two meetings."

"Right. Half the team will maintain security while I

meet with the rest. Then we'll switch and I'll go over everything for the rest. Lopez, I'm counting on you. Until Sonya is found, I want everyone on full alert. As far as the security team is concerned, the estate is under attack."

Sean looked at his watch. "I'll be there in ten minutes. Have the first team ready. And Lopez, I want you personally to intercept all phone calls to the estate. I want you on the phone when the kidnappers call. I have a feeling that call is coming in very soon."

Sean disconnected. He could count on Lopez. He'd been with Carlos ever since the businessman had come to the U.S. Lopez could have had Sean's job, but he didn't want it. He was a natural leader who'd been a guerrilla fighter in his youth. The security team respected Sean, but the fierce loyalty they felt for Lopez was what made them the best.

He glanced at the dashboard clock. It would take about an hour to brief the team, see Carlos, and discuss with Lopez how to handle the kidnappers' call when it came.

Then, as much as he hated it, he had to talk to Sophie. He growled in disgust as his body reacted in anticipation of seeing her. He wiped the vision of her lying in his bed from his brain and replaced it with the coy smile she'd given him as she'd gushed about loving danger.

Cleansing anger swept away his body's betraying arousal. She'd lied to him, penetrated his defenses.

How could he have been so weak? He'd never been one to lose his perspective because of a woman. Not

even his ex-wife. As much as he'd loved Cindy, he'd
known what she was.

But Sophie's sad eyes had gotten to him.

She'd followed him to the hospital this morning,
and he already knew those blue eyes didn't miss much.
He had to know what she'd seen.

# Chapter Seven

Sean parked in front of Weddings Your Way next to Sophie's little BMW. As he climbed out of his car, he pushed his sunglasses up to his forehead and squinted at the passenger side panel.

"What the hell?" A deep scratch marred the metallic red paint.

Alarm sent a shot of adrenaline through him. He walked around to the driver's side. The front fender was dented and traces of dark paint were embedded in the bent metal.

"Sophie." He looked toward the main doors of Weddings Your Way. In a few bounds, he was across the courtyard and up the steps. He pushed the door open and found himself face-to-face with Rafe Montoya.

"What the hell happened?" he demanded, his pugnacious stance daring Rafe to refuse to tell him. Out of the corner of his eye, he saw Sophie across the room. She turned, her hand rising to her throat.

"We've got a CSU on its way to process the car," Rafe said.

"Process—what happened?" He pushed past Rafe and stalked over to Sophie, who was standing next to a waifish young woman in tortoiseshell glasses.

As he approached, the waif stepped in front of Sophie. He probably looked like a raging bull, but he didn't care. His only concern was Sophie.

He ignored her petite protector. "What happened? Are you all right?"

Her blue eyes were filled with wariness and something he couldn't define, but she touched the smaller woman on the shoulder. "It's okay, Samantha," she said softly.

Samantha looked from Sophie to him, then patted Sophie's hand and retreated.

"Majors."

Montoya had followed him. Sean rounded on him.

"I'll be glad to fill you in on what happened."

"Yeah?" Sean clenched his fists. "Like you filled me in on the police commissioner's involvement? I think I'd rather talk to Sophie."

A glint of amusement lit Montoya's black eyes. "No doubt."

Sean bristled and took a step toward him.

"Rafe, please."

Sophie's voice brought Sean back from the edge of unreasoning anger.

"You two are like rams butting heads. I'll talk to Sean."

Montoya assessed her. Arching one dark brow, he held up a hand. "Fine, if you're sure."

She darted a glance at Sean. "I'm sure."

"I'll get your blouse to CSU, although they likely

won't be able to lift a print. They can analyze what the substance is, though."

Sophie nodded at him and avoided Sean's gaze.

As soon as Montoya had crossed the room, Sean bent his head and spoke softly. "I want to talk to you privately. Where can we go?"

When Sophie lifted her gaze to his, the wariness in her face, in her stance, made him feel like a bully. He took a deep breath and deliberately relaxed his tense muscles.

"Stop looking at me like that. I'm not going to hurt you. I just need to find out what happened."

Her expression told him she wasn't at all sure of him. Of course she wasn't. They barely knew each other.

Damn it, how had she stripped away his usual self-control? Even as he asked himself that question, he knew the answer. She fascinated him like no one he'd ever met. It didn't matter if she craved excitement and danger like his ex-wife. It didn't matter that he knew she was hiding something from him.

He'd made a huge mistake by inviting her into his home, and an even bigger one by inviting her into his bed.

When he'd discovered that she'd been abused, it had broken his heart. Combined with her vulnerable sexuality, she'd been impossible to resist. A surge of remembered ecstasy caused a hitch in his breathing.

She moistened her lips. "We can go out by the pool. It will be hot but…" Her voice trailed off and her gaze dropped to her hands.

"That's fine."

So she didn't know how to act after last night. Well, neither did he. All he knew was that he had to correct the mistake he'd made by giving in to his growing attraction for Sophie. He had to cut out his personal feelings. She didn't need his protection. She had Montoya to protect her.

The rest was just a matter of self-control.

There was too much at stake for him to be careless again. Besides, as he kept reminding himself, he had no time or inclination for a relationship.

Sophie led him through a set of French doors out to the pool area behind the main salon of Weddings Your Way. The day was hot, with a few white clouds floating lazily in the deep blue sky.

Beyond the opulent, tiled pool area was a magnificent view of the ocean. The fresh smell of salt water filled the air, and sunlight sparkled on the ocean's surface like floating diamonds.

Sophie led him around the pool to a white wrought-iron table and chairs covered by a gauzy canopy.

As they sat, his gaze lit on her legs and a splinter of compassion slipped into his heart. He gave his head a quick shake to dislodge the vision of the faded scars that crisscrossed her thighs and lifted his gaze to hers.

She blinked and looked down, fiddling with a button on her sleeve. "You wanted to ask me something?"

He rested one hand on the top of the table. He looked at it, then doubled it into a fist and bounced it lightly against the glass tabletop. His watchband clunked rhythmically.

Damn it, he had to do something to release the frustration and tension. If he paced, he wouldn't be able to watch her face.

"Let's see. Where do I start? How about telling me why you followed me to the hospital? Or why you pretended to be visiting your hospitalized cousin when my guard questioned you?"

He spread his fingers on the tabletop, then drummed them. "Or how about what the hell happened to your car? And when? Or why is your blouse being gone over for evidence?" He heard his voice growing harsher and louder. He swallowed and shrugged the tension out of his shoulders.

Sophie's eyes had grown wider as he'd thrown the questions at her. A breeze lifted her hair and blew it into her face. She tossed her head and moistened her lips. Then she clasped her hands in front of her on the table and looked down at them for a moment.

When she raised her head, her mouth was a tight line. She leaned forward and took a long breath.

"I followed you because I knew Rachel would want to know what had happened to Craig Johnson. I made up the story about the cousin because I needed a reason to be there. It was before visiting hours. I couldn't afford to be stopped and questioned."

Her knuckles turned white. "It turns out that it was a good thing. A man in blue surgical scrubs and a mask got onto the elevator with me." She shivered. "He watched me, all the way down to the lobby. Then he pushed everyone aside and darted down a side hall. I tried to follow him but he disappeared into an area marked 'Authorized Personnel Only.'"

"He pushed you?"

She nodded. "That's how I got the smear on my blouse. He wasn't a doctor. His fingernails and hands were dirty."

"Did he say anything?"

"No. He was just creepy. He never took his eyes off me."

"And you think—"

"I think he could be Johnson's murderer."

Sean stared at her as his mind struggled to comprehend. "If his hands were dirty, he had to have left fingerprints."

Frustration tightened his jaw. "I hope Montoya's men aren't destroying evidence."

"Our security team is the best."

Sean eyed her narrowly. "'Our' security team?"

Her eyelids fluttered. "Rachel's."

"Yeah. I find the amount of dollars and manpower devoted to security interesting for a wedding salon."

She pressed her lips together and averted her gaze.

"Can you describe the man?"

"I've told Rafe everything I can recall. We think he was the same man who tried to jab Samantha with a needle a couple of weeks ago. She noticed dirty fingernails, too."

"You said this guy boarded the elevator with you. That means he'd have to have been on the fourth floor when I left. I didn't see him."

Sophie shrugged. "He could have come up the stairs, or changed clothes."

Sean made a mental note to get Montoya to round up all hospital employees that fit Sophie's description and question them again.

He sat forward, too filled with anger and the need

for action to relax. "That explains the blouse. What about your car?"

"I drove home and showered—" She stopped. A blush painted her cheeks as her eyes met his.

For a brief instant, the night and their intimacy hovered between them, as palpable and substantial as a living thing. Her eyes glittered.

Sean wished he had the courage to reach for her, to touch her pink cheek and tell her it was all right. Her secret was safe with him. *All her secrets.* But that would bring him too close.

Her intrusion into his house, into his life, was too new, too raw. He needed distance right now. And he didn't have the courage to explain why.

He looked down.

After a beat, Sophie continued. "I changed clothes and drove back here. On the exit ramp, a car tried to run me into the guardrail." Her voice was steady but her knuckles were still white and the corners of her mouth were pinched.

"Damn, Sophie, are you all right?" A horrifying picture rose in his mind. Sophie's little red BMW convertible crushed between a big black monster of a car and the twisted metal of the guardrail.

A searing pain ripped through his heart, surprising the hell out of him. The idea of Sophie being hurt was unbearable.

She nodded.

He put his hand over her clasped ones. "Did you get the tag number? Did you call the police? Are you sure you weren't hurt?"

"I'm fine. I didn't catch the tag and, no, I didn't call the police."

The look on her face stopped him. "You reported it to Rachel Brennan instead."

He looked beyond her toward the palatial offices of Weddings Your Way. It was a facade, an illusion. Something else was going on here. Something that, if not sinister, was at least cloaked in secrecy, the kind of secrecy that only the government could manage.

Sophie said something.

"What?"

She shifted in her seat. "Nothing."

But he replayed what he'd heard in his head.

"Should have chased the car? Are you kidding me?" He shook his head at her. "No. You shouldn't have. They could have had guns. Sophie, was the driver trying to kill you?"

She didn't even blink at a question that should have floored her.

"I don't think so. It was a big car. If the driver had wanted to kill me, his car could have crushed mine with no effort. I think it was a warning."

"You were followed."

Sophie glanced at her watch and stood. "I'm sorry, Sean—Mr. Majors. I have an appointment with a client."

Sean stood, too. *Mr. Majors.* Apparently she regretted the night before as much as he did. Oddly, that didn't make him feel better.

"Sophie." He gripped her shoulder. "Someone followed you home. You know what that means."

She lifted her gaze to his.

"Your life is in danger."

"I can take care of myself," she said just as Montoya walked up. "Excuse me," she said quickly. "I'm sure my client is waiting."

Aware of Montoya's hooded gaze, Sean watched her walk back to the house. Her black skirt and pale gray blouse hugged her slender figure. She was beautiful and elegant and poised.

Sean wondered if the people she worked with knew all she'd overcome, all she'd sacrificed. He wondered if they knew how much effort it took for her to maintain her cool facade.

He couldn't help but wonder which Sophie was the real one. The sophisticated lady who'd just dismissed him, or the frightened young woman who'd responded so completely to him last night.

"You ready to be briefed?" Montoya asked him.

Sean didn't look at him. "You know the incident with the car was no accident."

Montoya didn't speak.

"She's in danger. They know where she lives."

"I'll protect her."

Sean faced the other man. "I'd feel better if I were the one protecting her."

Montoya laughed. "I'm sure you would."

"Don't underestimate me, Montoya. Like I told you, I make a better friend than enemy. Now, I want to see the crime-scene unit report on the evidence they found in Johnson's room."

JOSE FUENTES SAT in his car outside Sophie Brooks's apartment building, waiting for her. He hummed a Latin tune and beat out a salsa rhythm on the steering wheel. He had all the time in the world.

It had only taken a few minutes to take care of his primary job. He'd thrown the breaker, traced the electrical wiring, pulled it out and dropped it into position. That had left him ample time to explore her apartment. He figured it was one of the perks of his job.

He settled deeper into the driver's seat and closed his eyes as he relived the pleasure of running his rough fingers over her delicate underwear, of throwing back her bedclothes and smelling her scent on the sheets.

He loved getting that close to his female targets. Especially after the way she'd looked at him.

Man, that had pissed him off. She'd been suspicious of him, but her face had also reflected disgust and fear.

Still, she apparently didn't scare easily, because even after they'd roughed up her car, she hadn't hesitated to report his description to the authorities.

He and every other Hispanic male who worked at the hospital had been grilled all day today. And had scrapings taken from under their fingernails. It had been humiliating. Luckily, regular scrubbing was a hospital requirement. His nails might always appear dirty, but they'd get nothing from the scrapings.

He glanced at the dashboard clock. Eventually she would come home. She'd walk into her apartment, little suspecting that he'd been prowling through her things. Then slowly, she would realize that someone had been there, had touched her things, had violated her.

He planned to sit right there in his car and watch her windows as she walked through, turning on lights.

He looked forward to savoring each tiny sliver of doubt, each rising concern, that she'd feel as she began to realize that her things were not exactly as she'd left them.

She'd think she was wrong. Then she'd change her mind. He'd been very careful, very patient. He'd put everything back exactly as he'd found it.

He knew her type. He knew she'd notice. He also knew she'd doubt herself. If he'd judged her character correctly, she'd finally convince herself that she had no proof anyone had been in her apartment. She'd talk herself into believing it was her imagination, brought on by stress.

She'd feel uneasy, but she'd slowly relax. She'd make sure the apartment door was locked, and her windows were secure. She'd notice how tired she was. She'd try to unwind, maybe pour a glass of the wine he'd seen in her refrigerator.

And after the long, exciting day she'd had, she'd probably decide to take a shower.

Then she would die.

SOPHIE PARKED Rachel's Prius in front of her apartment and sighed. Thank goodness she was finally home. Rachel had been kind enough to loan her one of her cars and take her out to dinner, but the conversation had never wavered from two subjects.

What else could she remember about the events of the day, and Rachel's opinion of all the reasons Sean Majors was not the right man for Sophie.

She'd assured Rachel at least a dozen times that she wasn't interested in Sean, but the supercharged intuition that made Rachel a brilliant investigator didn't confine itself to criminals.

Sophie knew Rachel's intense blue eyes saw right through her lies.

Thankful to be home at last, Sophie stepped out of the car, locked it and headed for her apartment. She wanted a shower.

Her blouse was half unbuttoned by the time she'd locked the door behind her. As she sighed in relief to finally be home, her cell phone rang.

"Sophie, I didn't get to talk to you again. Are you okay?"

Sophie smiled as she set her purse down. It was Samantha. "I'm fine. Thanks for checking. Have you heard anything more about Johnson's death?"

"The crime-scene unit went over everything in the room. There were no smudges or fingerprints on Johnson's IV port, but Rafe said they found a pair of gloves with a faint smear on the *inside*. They were in the laundry chute, stuffed into a bag of towels and sheets."

"That makes sense. I couldn't figure out why the guy was dressed as a surgeon, but with no gloves. Were they able to lift a print or match the streak on my blouse?"

"I haven't heard. I was going to ask you the same thing. I heard you went to dinner with Rachel."

"She was sweet. Not her usual business persona." Sophie didn't want to tell Samantha about Rachel's motherly warnings about Sean.

"She's worried about you."

Sophie switched the cell phone to her other hand as she finished unbuttoning her blouse. "About me?"

"Come on, Soph. It's no secret that in the four years you've been here, you haven't dated at all."

"That's not true. I've been out."

"Right. Been out. Maybe twice. Everybody at Confidential worries about you."

A warm, alien sensation wrapped itself around Sophie's heart. It was the feeling of belonging. Her ingrained caution had kept her from becoming close to the other members of the Confidential Agency. But since she'd been shot at and nearly run down by the mysterious car, she'd experienced Rachel's worry, Rafe's protective attitude and now Samantha's friendly concern.

"You worry about me?" She gave a little laugh, feeling her cheeks burn. "Please tell me you guys don't sit around talking about my pathetic life."

Samantha laughed. "That's just it. You are so far from pathetic. You're gorgeous. You're smart. You need a man. Speaking of which, you were going to tell me more about Sean Majors. He's hot. You should latch on to him."

Sophie's face grew hotter. "Just because you've found your true love in Alex doesn't mean you have to match up every single male and female you know. Next, you'll be pairing up Isabelle and—and Rafe."

"It could happen. And by the way, you could do way worse than Sean Majors. But seriously, Sophie. Are you okay? Where are you?"

"I'm home, and about to take a shower. I've been up since five."

"I thought Rafe said the guy who smashed your car must have followed you from the hospital and knows where you live. You shouldn't be there alone. Why don't you stay at Weddings Your Way tonight?"

Sophie pushed aside the faint uneasiness caused by Samantha's concern. She'd been on her own since she was seventeen. She'd taken care of herself all her life.

"I've got my weapon. I've got double dead bolts on the doors, and I'm sure not going to let anyone in. I'll be fine."

"Still—"

"Samantha, you were with the FBI. Do you have any doubt that you can handle yourself?"

"No, but—"

"Well, I was CIA. Trust me. I know how to take care of myself."

"Okay, then. I guess I'll see you in the morning."

Sophie disconnected, a little surprised but relieved that Samantha had given in so quickly. She took her cell phone into the bathroom, then went into her bedroom to undress.

Opening her lingerie drawer, she reached for a pair of pink silk bikini panties. Her hand stilled. The three new pairs of panties she'd bought two weeks ago were under a bra.

She frowned. She'd been in a hurry this morning when she'd rushed home to shower and change after the excitement at the hospital—after spending the night with Sean. She'd probably moved the bra without realizing it.

She closed the drawer, then opened the one below it to retrieve her pajamas. They were folded neatly, just like she'd left them. When she picked them up, she spotted her peach silk camisole. It had several pulls in it.

She smoothed her hand over the delicate fabric. Had it been damaged in the wash? She certainly hadn't noticed that.

"This is your fault, Samantha," she muttered. "You've got me imagining things."

She glanced around the bedroom, just to assure herself that everything was in its place. The uneasiness that Samantha had raised grew to a flutter of apprehension under her breastbone. She hadn't felt so afraid since she was seventeen. She'd spent the past twelve years building a wall of invulnerability around herself. Nothing and no one would ever make her feel helpless and afraid again.

Closing her fist around the satin pj's, she shoved the drawer shut. She was tired, and her emotions were in turmoil because of the events of the past two days.

Just to be on the safe side, she unlocked her bedside table and retrieved her Glock and slapped a clip into it. It would probably be a good idea to carry it for the duration of the case. Then she double-checked the dead bolt on the front door. It was locked.

Expelling her unease with a long breath, she laid the Glock on the back of the toilet with her cell phone and slipped out of her skirt and stockings.

She pushed the shower curtain aside enough to turn on the hot water, closing her eyes in anticipation as the quickly warming water flowed over her hand.

In no time she had shed the last of her clothes and the bathroom was getting steamy.

She adjusted the water temperature a bit and stepped into the shower—just as thunderous banging filled the air.

She shot out of the shower stall as if someone had pushed her. Water dripped onto the floor. She froze, listening.

The banging started again.

Grabbing her pajama bottoms and the tank top, she wrestled them on over her wet body, then picked up her cell phone and her Glock. She stuck the cell phone into the pocket of the pajama bottoms.

She swiped wet hair out of her face with her forearm as she cautiously approached the front door, her weapon at the ready.

"Sophie!"

Her heart thudded into her throat. It sounded like—

"Who is it?" she shouted, pressing her back against the wall near the door with her weapon clutched in both hands.

"Sophie, it's Sean. Open up!"

*Sean.* Her breath caught. "What are you doing?"

"Open the damn door."

Had something happened? She lowered her weapon and turned the key in the two dead bolts, then unlocked the door.

He burst in without waiting for her to swing the door open.

She had to scramble out of his way.

"Sean, what's the matter? What are you doing here?"

His teal blue eyes quickly raked her from head to toe before he closed and locked the door.

"The question is what are *you* doing here?" His face was dark and contorted with rage.

Sophie took a step backward. "What's the matter with you? I live here," she shot back.

His gaze raked her again and stopped on the gun. A flicker of surprise lit his features.

She realized she was still holding it in both hands, the barrel pointed at the ceiling.

Then his gaze lowered to her breasts.

She glanced down. Her satin camisole was wet and plastered to her skin, outlining her nipples as plainly as if the hot pink had been painted on.

His gaze burned her skin, reminding her that he'd seen her breasts before, had touched them and kissed them and nipped and sucked them.

Her breasts and thighs tightened at the remembered feel of his mouth and hands, touching her in places she'd never allowed any man to touch.

*Damn.* Anger at herself for being susceptible to his presence fed her resentment that he'd barged in on her.

He took a step toward her.

She retreated.

"Does it mean nothing to you that the men who ran your car into the guardrail know where you live? That they could have been here waiting for you? What stupid notion made you come back here tonight?"

"Stupid? *Stupid?*" Sophie set the gun on a side table, hoping he'd forget about it. "This is my home. It's safe. Even if the car incident were connected with Johnson's death, which I'm not sure it was, why would they be after me? I can't identify the guy I saw."

"Why else would someone try to wreck your car?"

"Maybe I cut him off in traffic. Who knows?"

Sean shook his head, obviously frustrated. "Well, we're operating on the assumption that whoever the man was who you chased through the hospital considers you a threat. He had you followed, and the *car incident* was intended to scare you or kill you. So, no, you are not safe here. You need to stay somewhere else until this is over."

"Wait a minute. Samantha called you, didn't she?"

"No, why?"

Sophie propped her fists on her hips.

Sean rubbed his face. "Actually, it was Rachel Brennan. She's worried for your safety."

She thought about Rachel's warnings. "Rachel called *you* instead of Rafe? I don't believe it."

He nodded. "Believe it."

His gaze intensified until she thought it would burn a hole in her camisole. Her breasts ached to feel his warm fingers, his mouth. She swallowed a tiny moan.

He blinked, then lifted his eyes to hers. "Apparently Montoya is actually working with the *police* tonight. It's nice to know that he can."

"Rafe is very good at his job."

"So you've said. The question is, just what *is* his job? For that matter, what's yours?"

He was treading on dangerous ground. He'd been suspicious since the beginning. It was obvious Rachel hadn't told him anything, so Sophie had to keep him from uncovering Confidential's true identity and purpose.

She widened her eyes and ran her tongue along her lower lip, trying to appear excited at the prospect of someone spying on her. "Do you really think someone is out there, watching me?"

Sean's eyes narrowed for an instant and his jaw tightened. He was probably disgusted with her.

Finally, he shook his head. "I took a look around outside. I didn't see any suspicious vehicles, but that doesn't mean there's not someone out there. Did you notice anything odd when you got here? Anyone follow you? Anything out of place in your apartment?"

She hesitated for a fraction of a second, and he picked up on it as if he could read her mind.

"What is it? What happened?"

She shook her head, but he wrapped his hand around her elbow.

"Come on, Sophie. Stop acting so damned coy. You think I didn't notice how you held that Glock? You think I believe you learned to duck and roll like you did from a self-defense course?"

For an instant, Sophie wanted to confide in him, to lean on him. But she couldn't. If Rachel had wanted him to know about Confidential, she'd have told him herself.

"I don't know what you're hiding," he went on. "God knows you have a right not to trust anyone. But I'm trying to protect you. I don't—" He stopped and grimaced. "I don't want anything to happen to you," he muttered.

Sophie's pulse hammered in her throat. She didn't

know how to respond to his reluctant admission. She felt the pull of their attraction increase each time they met.

Did he? And if he did, was he fighting it as hard as she was? She'd never fit into his world, and he knew it.

"Okay. I had a feeling someone had been in here. Nothing I can point to. Just a sense that things weren't quite right." To her dismay, her voice quivered. She hoped he hadn't noticed.

But he had. He slid his hand up her arm to her neck and for the briefest instant, his fingers skimmed along her cheek like the caress of a lover.

For a second, she felt cherished, cared for.

"Are you sure? Nothing was out of place?" He took his hand away.

Sophie's eyes followed it. He had good hands. Strong. Gentle. She loved his hands.

"Sophie?"

"It seemed like some of my underwear was out of place, but I'm not that neat. I could have moved them myself."

"Show me."

Sophie shrugged and turned toward her bedroom, then heard the water running. "Oh. I left the shower on."

She headed toward the bathroom, acutely conscious of Sean behind her. Her pajama bottoms were as wet as her top, and she hadn't taken time to put on panties. She felt the wet material clinging to her every curve. She didn't dare reach back to peel it away from her skin.

In the steamy confines of her bathroom, Sean

stopped her with a hand on her shoulder. He slid around her to turn off the shower.

The muscles of his back undulated beneath his white polo shirt. She'd felt those muscles move under her palms. She knew the skin covering them was hot and smooth, unlike her scarred back. It was all she could do not to spread her fingers over the ridge of his spine.

"What's this?" His voice rang with alarm as the sound of the shower faded to silence.

"What's what?"

"Stand back." He turned his head toward her. "Get out of the bathroom."

She opened her mouth.

"Go!"

As she obeyed him and stepped out into the hall, he flung back the shower curtain and dug a high-powered miniature flashlight out of his pocket. He shone the beam toward the ceiling and from her position at the bathroom door, Sophie saw what he'd seen.

"What is that?"

He traced the black wires hanging down behind her shower caddy with the flashlight's beam. "Electrical wire. Hot."

Fear paralyzed her. She'd stepped into the shower stall with the water running full blast. If she'd reached for the soap or the shampoo, she might have been electrocuted.

"You were right about someone being in here. I'm calling the police." Sean backed out of the bathroom, retrieving his cell phone.

Sophie put her hand over his.

He glanced up, fear and anger etched into the lines of his face.

"Call Rafe."

A flash of irritation crossed his features, but he paused, then shook his head. "Fine. I don't guess it would do me any good to ask you why."

He didn't wait for her answer. He just dialed Rafe's number and spoke to him.

"She's fine," he said. "Right. I'm planning to." He paused. "Don't worry. I will."

He disconnected. "Get some clothes on. I need to get you out of here. I'm taking you to Carlos's estate for the night."

*Not to his apartment.*

She was shocked at herself. Why was that her first thought? She should be grateful that he'd been here. That he'd showed up when he had. She shuddered to think of what could have happened if she'd touched that wire.

But the fact that he would take her all the way to the Botero estate rather than to his apartment was like a slap to her face.

He didn't want her around his daughter. Around him.

It shouldn't bother her, she told herself. It shouldn't matter. She'd spent most of her life making sure people couldn't hurt her. But for some reason, Sean's obvious regret over taking her to his home dug deep into her heart, wounding her in a way she hadn't allowed herself to feel in years.

She lifted her chin. "I have Rachel's Prius. I'll go to Weddings Your Way. There are sleeping quarters there."

"I'll take you."

"No. I'll drive. Don't you need to stay here and wait for Rafe?"

Sean clenched his fists and his face darkened. "Montoya will handle the crime scene. He asked me to make sure you're safe."

"It seems everyone is putting that burden on you tonight. Well, I can assure you it's not necessary. There's plenty of security at Weddings Your Way."

"Did you somehow miss the obvious fact that you came within an inch of being killed tonight?"

Sean's voice was raspy with emotion. His face still reflected anger, and when he'd been talking to Rafe, Sophie had noticed that his hand had been shaky.

Everything from the past two days came rushing into her mind like a flash flood. The shooting at the ransom drop, the emotion-laden meeting with Sean's daughter and the heart-wrenching experience of making love with Sean afterward. The encounter with Johnson's suspected murderer, and the car that had tried to run her into the guardrail.

Now danger had followed her into her own apartment. Someone had tried to kill her. She began to tremble.

"Yes, it has occurred to me, thank you," she said coldly. "I'll be fine at Weddings Your Way. You don't have to worry about me."

"I'll follow you," he insisted.

"Fine." She lifted her chin a fraction higher. "I'll get my purse."

To her surprise, Sean's face relaxed in a crooked smile. "It might be better if you put some clothes on."

Her face burned as her hand flew to cover her breasts. "Right. I'll do that. Now."

She fled into her bedroom.

FUENTES WAS SURPRISED to see Sophie come out of her apartment. When he'd seen Botero's security chief drive up, he'd sunk down in the driver's seat, hoping the man hadn't seen him. He might have had to shoot him.

But after surveying the parking lot for a few moments, he'd knocked on Sophie's door. Fuentes had smiled. He knew no one could trace him to the exposed wires in the shower, and who knew, maybe he'd kill two birds with one stone, so to speak. Maybe Sophie and her lover would shower together.

But now Sophie was alive and well, and headed for the little Prius, and Botero's security chief got into his own car.

Well, there was more than one way to solve the problem of the inquisitive blonde. It didn't matter to him if she was dead or just scared to death. Just so long as she didn't make a positive identification of him.

He picked up his cell phone and spoke with an accomplice, giving him directions and a description of Sophie's car. Then he started his car and pulled out behind the security chief, careful to stay far enough back that the man wouldn't know he was being followed.

Care and patience. That was the key. He just hoped his buddy would be as careful. With any luck, Sophie would be gone tonight. But even if tonight's plan didn't work, there was always tomorrow. Sophie would come back to her apartment for a shower eventually.

## Chapter Eight

Sean followed Sophie, silently cursing her for driving so fast. Was she trying to lose him? Surely she wasn't planning to give him the slip and go somewhere other than Weddings Your Way.

He sped up, maneuvering around vehicles until he was right behind her. Traffic wasn't too bad now. Earlier, on his way to Sophie's apartment after Rachel Brennan's call, it had been heavy.

He glanced at the dashboard clock. Ten o'clock. Rachel had called around eight-thirty. At least he'd had a chance to play with Michaela and read her a bedtime story. And thank goodness for Rosita. She complained constantly—always had, even when she was his nanny. But she adored Michaela, and she knew the nature of Sean's business meant that he often kept late hours. She never minded sleeping over with his daughter.

Sophie pulled ahead again. They were only two exits away from Weddings Your Way. Sean saw the fine shape of her head silhouetted against the streetlights. She was beautiful.

In fact tonight, with no makeup on and her hair and those slinky pajamas plastered to her wet skin, she was the sexiest, most gorgeous thing he'd ever laid eyes on. She'd shed the sophisticated persona and looked vulnerable and soft, like she had in his bed.

The contradiction of her wet and shivering body and that Glock, which she held as if she'd been born with it in her hands, had been an excruciating turn-on.

His frustration at being called out to check on her by Rachel, and his anger at Sophie for going back to her apartment even though she *knew* someone had followed her, had dissolved into lust when she'd opened the door.

Her face had reflected genuine surprise, and those wide blue eyes had suckered him in, just like they always did.

A black car cut in front of him, separating him from Sophie and jerking his thoughts back to the present. He pulled into the left-hand lane, but the car zipped back over in front of him.

"What the hell?" He tried to make out the license plate but the light was out and the plate was smeared with mud.

Ahead of him, the Prius was pulling away.

Sean jerked the wheel and veered back into the far right lane, speeding up.

The black car pulled up beside him, so close it almost scraped his bumper. He glanced sideways, but the windows were darkly tinted. Flooring the accelerator, he pulled ahead.

Where was Sophie? Suddenly the interstate seemed crowded.

There she was, three cars ahead. A mid-sized dark blue Ford pulled up beside her and swerved toward her.

He cursed and glanced in the side mirror. The black car was gaining on him. He kept his foot pressed to the floor.

The Ford scraped the side of the Prius.

Sean's heart thudded against his chest wall.

*Come on,* he urged his car. *Move!* He was gaining on the two vehicles.

The Ford veered away, then swerved back.

Sean cringed as Sophie jerked the Prius to the right, onto the shoulder. The Ford closed in on her, keeping pace with her speed.

Sean leaned on his horn as he passed an SUV.

The Prius wobbled on the rough pavement. He saw the brake lights come on as Sophie tried to escape the sedan by slowing down.

"Good move, Sophie."

But it didn't work. The Ford slowed, too, and continued to crowd the little Prius.

Then the right side of Sophie's front fender caught the guardrail and swung sideways, out into traffic.

Horns blared and brakes squealed as vehicles dodged the little car. The Ford took off with a burst of speed.

Sean watched in horror as the little Prius twirled around and around like a top, its tires squealing and sliding on the pavement.

He braked, maneuvering toward the wildly spinning car, hoping that he could figure out some way to stop the inevitable crash.

Time slowed around him as he watched helplessly. Later, he would remember a vague awareness that the black car had disappeared. But now all that mattered was that Sophie was inside the out-of-control Prius. She could be killed or horribly injured, and he could do nothing but watch it unfold like a video in slow motion.

The Prius finally stopped turning, facing traffic, and slid sideways into the guardrail with the deafening screech of crushing metal.

"No!" Sean couldn't breathe. His heart had stopped beating.

He stood on his brakes. His car came to a screaming halt about four feet from the mangled metal of the Prius.

"Oh no! Please, God, please—"

He threw himself out of the driver's seat and ran to Sophie. The Prius had turned completely around, crashing the passenger side into the concrete-and-metal guardrail. The entire length of that side of the car was crushed, and steam was escaping from under the hood.

He steeled himself. He'd seen death and injury before. He'd knelt beside a fellow soldier, trying to stop the flow of blood from the boy's chest with his hands. The soldier hadn't made it. Sean had spent the rest of the day covered in the dead boy's blood.

But if Sophie was dead—if her beautiful scarred body was broken—

Sean shook his head to rid his eyes of the haze of tears. His heart hammered in his chest. It surprised him. He'd thought it had stopped.

The only thing he saw through the driver's window was the air bag. He wiped his eyes with his palms and clenched his jaw, then reached out and yanked on the door handle.

It opened.

He took a deep breath that caught at the top like a sob. Retrieving a small knife from his pocket he popped the air bag.

As the white fabric collapsed like a balloon, he pushed it out of the way.

*Sophie.* She was slumped over the seat belt strap that held her in place. Her eyes were closed and her head lolled on her chest.

"Sophie." His lips moved, but his throat was paralyzed with fear. No sound escaped.

"Sophie," he said again, raspily.

Nothing.

He placed shaking fingers on her neck, searching for a pulse, praying to feel the swish of blood under that delicate skin.

She moaned.

His breath whooshed out in an audible sigh. He laughed shakily, nervously as his eyes filled with tears.

*She was alive.*

"Sophie, talk to me. Are you hurt?" He scanned her body, pushing away more of the deflated air bag, looking for blood. Her legs looked okay.

He lifted her chin and saw a huge red mark over her left brow. Her eyelids fluttered and she stared up at him, wide-eyed.

"Sean, I ran off the road," she whispered. "My hand hurts."

"Sophie, if I unbuckle your seat belt, can you stand?"

She never took her eyes off him. "I don't know." She blinked slowly. "Am I bleeding?"

He cradled her head, noticing that her hair was still damp. "I don't think so, but we'll check. Where do you hurt?"

Closing her eyes, she frowned. "My head. My hand. Everything."

Sean leaned over and unbuckled the seat belt. "Let's get you out of here."

A car stopped behind them. Sean stiffened, then straightened up and reached behind his back, closing his fist around the butt of his gun.

The man came running over. "Everything okay? Need help?"

"I think we're okay," Sean said, relaxing his hand. "Could you call 911?"

"Sure thing." The man peered inside the Prius. "Anybody else in there?"

Sean shook his head. "I think her injuries are minor, but tell them to send the EMTs just in case."

"No problem, bud," the man said, pulling out his cell phone.

Sean noticed other cars slowing and stopping, but he left it to the good Samaritan to let them know that the accident was a minor one.

When he turned back to Sophie, she was beginning to carefully move her body.

"Here," he said. "Let me help."

"No. I'm okay." She lifted her right hand, then cried out sharply and froze. Her face drained of color.

"What is it?"

"My—hand—" She gasped.

Sean looked down at it. There was an odd bump on the back, and it was turning purple. He touched it gently with a finger but she cried out again so he stopped. "I think it may be broken."

She nodded slightly, her lips pressed together, their corners white. "I feel sick."

"Just lean your head back. The EMTs will be here any minute." As he spoke, sirens wailed in the distance. "Any second."

She obediently put her head back against the seat. "What happened?"

"Just exactly what I expected might happen. A car ran you off the road—again."

Sophie opened one eye to a slit. "Believe it or not, I know that. I was there. When the fender hit the guard-rail, the air bag deployed. I guess it knocked me out, because that's the last thing I remember."

"You spun around about four times before slamming into the rail."

"No wonder I feel dizzy."

Sean brushed her hair back from her face, careful not to touch the darkening bruise on her brow. "You feel dizzy because the air bag gave you a black eye."

Her eyes flew open and her left hand gingerly touched her head. She winced. "I need to get out of here." She tried to sit up, but Sean stopped her with a hand on her shoulder.

"Wait. The EMTs are here."

Just as he spoke, the ambulance pulled up in front of the Prius and a man dressed in white rushed over carrying an emergency kit. "Got an injury here?"

Sean squeezed Sophie's shoulder and got out of the way. A police car was headed toward them, so Sean quickly took out his cell phone and dialed Montoya.

"I don't have time to talk," he said as soon as Montoya answered. "Someone ran Sophie off the road. She's bruised and shaken, but I think she's okay. The police are here."

To his credit, Montoya didn't waste any words. "Can you play it as an accident?"

"On one condition."

"Yeah?"

"That you tell me what's going on."

"Look, Majors—"

A middle-aged officer walked up. Even though the streetlights were bright, the officer held his flashlight at shoulder level.

"Gotta go. The police are here."

He flipped his phone shut.

"What happened here? Is the driver okay?"

Sean glanced at Sophie, who was being helped out of the car by the EMT. She cradled her right hand against her chest, and wobbled as she tried to stand. The EMT held her left elbow to steady her. She finally nodded, and the two of them walked slowly toward the open ambulance door.

His cell phone, which he still held in his hand, rang. He flipped it open and looked at the caller ID. It was Montoya. He didn't answer it.

The officer shone his flashlight at Sean's face. "Sir, I asked what happened."

Sean knew what he did in the next few seconds could

affect Rachel Brennan's agenda. She was obviously working with the police commissioner. He hadn't forgotten the commissioner's words.

*Trust us. There are some very touchy international matters.... We have no choice but to maintain a low profile.*

He took a deep breath and met the police officer's impatient gaze.

"I was following Ms. Brooks in my car when a dark blue Ford sideswiped her. She lost control. The other car didn't even slow down. It's possible he didn't even know she'd crashed." Sean swallowed the bitter taste of lies. "It was an accident."

"IS THERE ANYTHING else you need?" Sean stood at the door of one of the guest suites of Carlos Botero's mansion, trying not to be affected by Sophie. She looked so small and vulnerable in a white T-shirt of his that didn't quite make it to mid-thigh.

Her feet were bare, and a wrist brace decorated her right hand. The bruise over her eye was turning dark blue.

She shook her head. "Whose T-shirt is this?"

"It's mine. I keep a change of clothes here, in case I have to stay overnight." He glanced at his watch. During the past two hours, he'd given a statement to the police that contained so many lies and omissions it was worthy of prosecution.

He'd called Rosita to check on Michaela, filled Montoya in on the team effort to kill Sophie and picked her up at the emergency room and driven her to Carlos's estate, ignoring her protests.

He was tired. He needed sleep. And so did she.

"Are you staying overnight tonight?"

He shook his head.

"You're leaving me here alone in Botero's estate? Does he even know I'm here? Does anyone?"

"I don't bother Mr. Botero with trivial matters. His nurse and the security staff know you're here. You'll be safe, and well taken care of."

"Trivial matters. I see."

Sean winced. He hadn't meant it like that. "Mr. Botero is very ill. He's waiting to hear something about his daughter. I don't want him to know that people are being targeted."

She nodded, then touched her head with her left hand. "I think I've got to lie down."

Sean reached her side in two long strides and slid an arm around her waist. "Did they give you pain medication at the emergency room?"

"An injection. I feel sick."

Her body shook, and her skin felt clammy. "It was probably some form of codeine or morphine. When did you last eat?"

She didn't say anything for a couple of seconds. "Maybe lunch?"

"No wonder you can't stand up."

He yanked back the covers on the king-size bed with his free hand. He hadn't told her this was the suite he used when he stayed overnight. That hadn't happened many times. Most recently was the night Sonya had been kidnapped.

He helped her sit, then watched as she lay down and

stretched out her long, shapely legs. Reluctantly, he covered them.

She sighed and closed her eyes.

He picked up the phone. "What do you want to eat?"

She shook her head slightly. "Nothing. I don't feel like eating."

The cook's sleepy voice answered the phone. "Cook, sorry to bother you, but can you fix a plate of cheese and crackers and a pot of herbal tea and bring it to my room? Thanks."

"Sophie, I need to ask you a few questions while we're waiting for the food. The police questioned you at the scene. What did you tell them?"

"Nothing. I said it was an accident."

"Did you mention the blue Ford?"

"The officer asked me about it, so I said it side-swiped me. That's all."

"Good. That's what I told them. Now—" he sat down on the edge of the bed, facing her "—did you get the license plate? Did you see the guy? Anything?"

His cell phone rang, interrupting him. It was Montoya.

"Montoya."

"Why haven't you answered any of my calls? How's Sophie? What happened with the police?"

"Sophie's all right. She has a badly sprained wrist, not broken as I'd suspected, and a nasty-looking bruise on her forehead. And a black eye. We just got back from the emergency room."

"Where are you?"

"At Carlos's estate. She's staying here tonight."

"What about the police?"

"They think it was a hit-and-run. That the car side-swiped Sophie and took off."

"Let me talk to her."

Sean surveyed her pale face and the shadows beneath her closed eyes. "She's pretty groggy. They gave her pain medication."

"Have her call me in the morning, then. And Majors—"

"Yeah?"

"Be sure she's safe."

"Don't worry. That's right at the top of my priority list."

"Speaking of priorities, have you heard anything from the kidnappers?"

"No, and I don't like it. It's been too long."

A discreet knock on the door announced Cook's arrival. She came in and placed the tray on the foot of the king-size bed.

Sean nodded at her and she left.

"You don't think Botero has heard something and is keeping it from you, do you?"

"That's impossible. Javier, his nurse, is with him twenty-four hours a day. Plus, Carlos doesn't have a cell phone. I can be patched into any call that comes into this house. My people have very specific instructions about what to do if the kidnappers call. Trust me. There's been no word."

Montoya was silent for a beat. "What do you think that means?"

Sean didn't miss the concern in Montoya's voice. It

was the same concern that had been plaguing him all day. Why hadn't the kidnappers called? For his boss's sake, he prayed Sonya was still alive.

"I wish I knew."

He pulled the tray of food closer and poured a cup of fragrant, steaming tea for Sophie, who took it gratefully, wrapping her left hand around the warm cup.

"Let's meet tomorrow, and discuss strategy."

Sean frowned. "Let's meet tomorrow and discuss who Rachel Brennan is, and who you really work for."

Sophie sent him a sidelong glance as she reached for a cracker with her braced hand. She snagged one between two fingers.

Montoya's derisive laugh echoed through the wireless connection. "I'll discuss it with Rachel, but she doesn't respond well to threats."

"No threat. I thought we had a deal."

"You stated your condition. I never agreed."

"Give it a rest, Montoya. We're on the same side."

"I'll talk to you tomorrow."

As he disconnected, Sophie reached for another cracker.

"Are you going home?" she asked.

"Yes. My daughter expects to see me when she wakes up."

"Michaela." Sophie smiled. "She's so lucky to have you as her daddy."

"I'm lucky to have her," he said, hearing the sadness in her voice and picturing the scars on her back and legs.

Anger surged through him. If he could reach back

through the years, he'd turn the tables on the bully who'd inflicted so much pain on Sophie.

Sophie opened her eyes. "She has your eyes and your determined jaw."

Anger of another kind swept through him. "Yeah. Well, that's up for debate."

He pulled up the coverlet and smoothed it over Sophie's slight form. "You need to rest."

"You don't want to talk about her with me." Sophie's voice was tentative, sleepy.

When he lifted his gaze to hers, her eyes were closed.

"I'm so sorry, Sean. I should have gone on. I never should have come up to your apartment. I didn't mean to invade your private space."

Her eyes drifted open and a sweet smile lit her face. "But I wouldn't trade the world for the opportunity to meet Michaela. She's so beautiful. So perfect. How could anyone ever leave her? At least she knows you'll always be there."

Sean studied Sophie's face. Her expression was soft and shadowed with loneliness and sorrow.

"How could anyone have left you?" That had slipped out. But even as his brain flashed warning signals, he leaned forward and gently kissed her bruised forehead.

She turned her head, making it impossible for him to ignore her luscious, full lips. He slid his mouth down her temple, her cheek, her jaw, until he'd traced a path from her forehead to her lips.

Her breath caught as his lips brushed against hers. The little sound told him his kisses stirred her, and that sent him into rigid, pulsing hardness. He touched her throat and the underside of her jaw as he deepened the kiss, tasting her lips, urging them apart to slip his tongue inside. She moaned and opened her mouth, accepting his intimate probing.

He wanted her desperately, totally. His brain was fogged with passion. His arousal throbbed painfully against the constricting denim of his jeans.

Running his hand down over her breasts, he felt them tighten under the thin material of the T-shirt that was her only clothing. He touched and squeezed each taut nipple and was rewarded when her back arched upward, pushing her breasts against his hand.

He placed one hand on either side of her to brace himself as he took her mouth in a deep, mind-numbing kiss, then trailed his tongue down her neck. He bent his head to find the hard peak of one breast. As he nipped at it and slid one hand down to the hem of the T-shirt, her arm came up and the stiff plastic of her wrist brace scraped his neck.

He froze. *What the hell was he doing?* Did he think he could make love to her in Carlos's house, while his daughter slept, secure in the belief that her daddy was at home? Did he think Sophie had changed, just because she was hurt? He still couldn't trust her—professionally or personally.

If she was like his ex-wife—

Sophie opened her heavy-lidded eyes and frowned. "Sean..." she whispered.

He straightened, wishing he could pretend nothing had happened. Wishing he could go back in time for two minutes and resist her vulnerable beauty.

"I assume you've had your fill of excitement for one day," he said dryly as he looked at his watch. "I'm going home. If you need anything during the night, press Star Four on the phone. That's the night security guard. He can contact Javier, the nurse."

He turned toward the door.

"Sean?"

Her voice held that tentative note that always got to him. "Yeah?"

"Thank you. I'm grateful that you were following me."

He looked back at her. "Even though you tried to lose me in traffic?"

She blushed.

"Maybe one day you'll be grateful enough to tell me the truth."

She put a lot of effort into not reacting. "The truth?"

"Who you are, and what organization the Weddings Your Way facade is covering up."

He left, gratified by the look of guilty surprise on her face.

# Chapter Nine

The next morning, Sophie awoke to the sound of her bedroom door opening. She automatically reached toward her bedside table where she kept her gun, but a shooting pain in her wrist stopped her.

She wasn't in her apartment. Sean had brought her to Carlos Botero's estate.

"Beg your pardon, ma'am, but Mr. Majors left word for you to be woken up at nine o'clock. Cook sent you breakfast."

Sophie yawned as the maid put a large tray down on the unused side of the bed. The combined scents of coffee, fresh rolls and bacon swirled around her, helping her wake up. She looked at the foot of the bed. The tray from the night before was gone.

"He also asked me to find you something to wear."

"Why? Where are my clothes?"

"Mr. Majors said to have them cleaned. I've laundered your underwear. It's here with the dress. Mr. Majors said to find you something long." The maid held up a loose, flowing rayon dress in a soft pale blue.

*Something long.* A twinge of appreciation squeezed Sophie's heart. He'd known she'd want something to cover her legs.

"Thank you," she said. "That's a beautiful dress."

"It was—is—Miss Sonya's."

Sophie eyed the young maid. Was referring to Sonya in the past tense just a slip of the tongue? Or something more sinister?

The girl's eyes filled with tears. "Pardon me, ma'am." Her lower lip trembled.

"You're worried about Sonya?"

"Yes, ma'am. She was always so good to me. To all of us. I hope—" The girl couldn't go on.

Sophie didn't think it was an act. The young maid truly believed that Sonya might already be dead. "What's your name?"

"Amelia, ma'am."

"Amelia, Mr. Majors and the people I work for are doing everything we can to get Sonya back safely. If you hear or see anything that might help us, you let Mr. Majors know, okay?"

"Yes. Okay. Thank you, ma'am."

After the maid had left, Sophie dressed as quickly as she could, considering the wrist brace.

The dress was a little large in the bosom, but otherwise it fit nicely, though it only came to slightly below her knees. She was sure it was mid-calf or longer on Sonya.

Wishing she had some stockings, she slipped her feet into the black, medium-heeled sandals she'd worn the night before.

She sat on the bed and poured a cup of coffee and buttered a roll. It occurred to her that she was hungry. After downing the roll in a few bites, she took a second cup of coffee awkwardly in her left hand and stood at the window, looking out over the immaculately kept grounds.

This was Carlos Botero's estate. She thought about the old man, sick and plagued with fear for his daughter's life. She thought about all the people working to find Sonya.

If she were kidnapped, no one would pay her ransom. No one would wait helplessly, hopefully, to hear whether she was alive.

"Stop it," she whispered to herself. "You're being maudlin. You know you're just not family material." Her brain fed her a vision of Sean and his daughter, laughing together.

She smiled, and her eyes stung.

A sharp knock on the door startled her. She turned and set the cup down on the table beside the window as the door opened.

It was Sean. He was dressed in a summer-weight blue suit and looked like a young executive.

His eyebrows shot upward as he took in her appearance. "Wow. You look—different."

"Thanks. It's my new look—no makeup, a borrowed dress and shoes that don't match."

He stared at her until she squirmed in discomfort. "Well, it works. I like the color."

"Do you?" She looked down at herself. "I never wear blue."

"It—" He paused. "It brings out the color of your eyes."

Suddenly uncomfortable, she crossed her arms. "I meant to ask for a sweater."

"A sweater? Why?"

"No sleeves." She chafed her upper arms, her face turning pink with embarrassment.

"Oh, right," Sean said as comprehension dawned in his eyes. "Let me see."

He stepped close behind her and positioned her so the sun shone on her right arm. Sophie stood immobile as he ran a gentle finger down the armhole of the dress. He examined her bare shoulder, touching a place here and there. Then he turned with her, so her left shoulder was illuminated in sunlight, and did the same thing.

When he touched the ugly scar the heavy belt buckle had left, her skin tightened and she shivered.

"This is the only one that shows," he murmured, smoothing his thumb over the tiny ridge.

Sophie's whole body tightened in reaction as she recalled the feel of his hot body pressed against hers and his lips brushing the scar.

"It looks beautiful to me. But we could put a Band-Aid on it, or you could tell people a kid in grade school threw a stick at you."

Sophie grimaced and blinked rapidly to stop the tears that were threatening to fill her eyes. Nobody had ever treated her so considerately. She'd never let anyone close enough before.

And she couldn't now. Letting him make love to her, letting him in, was a mistake.

*Not family material.* She pulled away, out of his grasp. "Thanks," she said shortly. "The stick story should work."

Sean dropped his hands and let Sophie retreat. If she hadn't moved, he'd have bent his head and kissed her scarred shoulder. He couldn't believe how hard it was to keep his hands off her. Almost as hard as it was to hang on to his belief that she was too much like his ex-wife.

"Are you ready to go?" he asked.

"Are we going to Weddings Your Way? I want to hear everything. What did Rafe find at my apartment? Were they able to glean any evidence from the Prius?"

Sean held up his hands. "Whoa. One thing at a time. Yes, we're going to Weddings Your Way. I need to be briefed on everything that's happened too. Are you ready?"

His cell phone buzzed. He glanced at the caller ID. It was his security guard, Kenner. "Kenner, what is it?"

"Kidnappers are on the line, sir."

"Where is Carlos?"

"In the study."

"I'm on my way. Patch me through." He swung around and sprinted through Sophie's open door and down the hall toward the study. He heard the click of her heels on the Italian marble floor behind him.

There was a buzzing on the line, then he heard Carlos's voice.

"Please, tell me my daughter is alive."

"Just listen up, old man, or you'll never see her again."

Sean burst into the study and waved a hand at Carlos, gesturing to him to stop talking.

"This is Sean Majors, Mr. Botero's chief of security. Mr. Botero is too ill to speak with you."

"What the hell? He was just talking."

Sean mouthed the word *cough* at Carlos, then met Javier's gaze. Javier nodded and leaned down to whisper in Carlos's ear.

Carlos started coughing.

"You'll have to talk to me." Sean waited. Were the kidnappers anxious enough to deal with him rather than Botero?

Out of the corner of his eye, he saw Sophie walk over to the desk and whisper to Carlos. The old man looked up at her for a moment, then nodded. She took the portable telephone handset from him and held it to her ear.

Sean frowned.

"Botero better get to feeling better soon," the voice on the phone said. "Because if he doesn't personally make the drop this time, we'll ship his lovely daughter home in a box, or maybe two or three boxes." The man laughed.

"He'll be there. When? Two hours from now?"

"Oh, no. No, no, no. The plans have changed. I will call you again. Meanwhile, you'd better get to work, because the price has also changed. It has doubled. This time, it is four million."

Sean grimaced, his pulse racing. "Wait. You have to give us time to get the money together."

"You should have thought ahead. Mr. Chief of Security. You should have expected the price to go up, since you disobeyed our instructions last time."

He met Sophie's gaze. "How did we disobey? We were there. We left the money in the designated place. You didn't even pick it up."

"I was too busy counting the sharpshooters you had surrounding me. When we say alone, Mr. Majors, that is what we mean."

"I understand."

"Do you also understand that I am a man of my word? I have promised you that Botero will have his daughter back, maybe alive, maybe dead. Would he like a part of her back as a gesture of my sincerity? A thumb, perhaps?" The speaker laughed again.

"No!" Sean took a deep breath. "That won't be necessary. I will carry out your instructions. When will we hear from you again?"

"Whenever I please. Goodbye, Mr. Sean Majors, Chief of Security."

Sean held his breath, but all he heard was dead air.

"They're gone," Sophie said, turning the handset off and setting it on Carlos's desk. "Do you think they'd really—"

"Javier," Sean interrupted before Sophie could voice the grotesque suggestion the kidnapper had presented.

He sent her a warning glance as he pocketed his cell phone. "We need to be prepared, in case Mr. Botero needs to go out this afternoon."

He sat on his heels in front of Carlos. "Sir, do you think you can go to the ransom drop? It could be today or tomorrow. They wouldn't give me a time."

"Anything. Anything for my Sonya." Botero's hands gripped the armrests of his wheelchair. "None of this would have happened if Sonya had listened to me. Where is that bastard DeLeon? This is all his fault. I ought to serve the kidnappers his head on a platter."

Carlos began coughing in earnest. Sean nodded at Javier, who started preparing a mild sedative.

"I'm doing everything I can to find Sonya. As soon as we hear from the kidnappers, we'll be ready. We'll do what they ask, and we won't call in the police."

Carlos nodded.

Sean rose and gestured to Sophie to follow him out of the room. It irritated the hell out of him that she'd listened in on the kidnappers' call. And the reason it bothered him irritated him even more.

There was a battle raging inside him. He wanted to believe that she was just like his ex-wife. An adrenaline junkie. That would make it easy to break the spell she'd cast over him. Or it should. It should also make him stop wanting to protect her and shield her from hurt.

On the other hand, he wanted to believe she was different. That her claim about loving the danger was a smokescreen hiding her real purpose. That the sadness in her eyes was real.

Either she was a thrill-seeker, or she was lying to him. Neither choice was acceptable. So why couldn't he stop thinking about her?

"Sean, wait."

He looked up to see her rushing down the front steps to catch up with him, the pale blue dress and her blond hair making her look as if she'd stepped out of a watercolor painting.

He'd walked all the way through the large foyer and out to his car without realizing it.

*Damn it.* It was her fault. She was a distraction. Her

presence interfered with his ability to do his job. He should be thinking about the kidnappers and trying to figure out a way to stay one step ahead of them, not chauffeuring Sophie around the city.

He got into his car and started it. She walked around to the passenger side and reached for the door handle. It was locked.

With ill grace, Sean pressed the unlock button.

She climbed in.

Neither of them spoke as Sean drove past the guardhouse and headed toward the interstate. He pulled out his cell phone.

Sophie watched his hand as he punched in a number and held the phone to his ear.

"Winstead," he said. "Got a complication. Yeah. We need another two million."

He scowled as he listened to the man on the other end of the phone.

"I know. But you've got to get on it. They could call at any time. Twice as heavy. I know that. Just get it. Any denomination. Call me when it's ready."

He snapped the phone shut and glanced at Sophie. "Botero's money manager," he said unnecessarily.

But his comment broke the silence between them and opened a connection. Sophie half turned in her seat. "Thank you for thinking about my clothes."

He shrugged it off.

"I mean it. You were very thoughtful. The long skirt, I mean. You have a lot on your mind, and so much has happened in the past twenty-four hours. Johnson dying, two near misses on the highway, my apartment booby-trapped. Oh, my gosh!" Sophie's stomach turned over. "I hadn't realized—since Johnson died, everything has been aimed at me."

"Finally picked up on that, eh? At least you're getting your wish. I'd think *anyone* would have gotten their fill of excitement and danger by now."

His bitter tone scraped across her sensitized nerves. She wanted to shake him, to kiss him, to put her arms around his neck and swear to him that she was nothing like his wife. But it wouldn't change his mind about her.

And anyway, it would be a lie.

So she leaned back in her seat and uttered a tight little laugh. "Last night was plenty of both. But why? Why are they targeting me?"

Sean's teal blue eyes sent her a disbelieving look. "How about because you rode in the elevator with the man who murdered Johnson? You are the only person who knows who he is."

"But that's just it. I *don't* know who he is. I don't know anything. He had a mask over his face."

"You chased him. He knows you were suspicious of him. So he's decided to silence you."

Sophie nodded, her throat constricting at the permanence of the word *silence*. She swallowed. "I get that. What I don't get is why. If he'd just lie low, he'd probably never be caught."

"I don't think he can afford to lie low. I think he may be a major player in this ransom game."

"You think he has Sonya?"

Sean shook his head. "No, but I think he knows where she is."

"Sean, I doubt I could identify him, even if we were face-to-face."

"You said he had a scar."

"Across his brow, as if he'd been in a fight. It looked old."

"There you go. An identifying mark. You told Montoya and the police, right?" Sean turned into the Weddings Your Way parking lot and cut his engine.

"Of course. In fact, I wonder why I haven't been called to do a lineup."

"That is a good question." He got out of the car, rounded it and opened her door.

She pulled the skirt of Sonya's dress down over her bare knees and got out.

Sean's hand rested just above her hip as they walked up to the door. It was warm, strong, protective.

Ironic that within the past twenty-four hours, her life had been threatened three times, yet the same twenty-four hours with Sean at her side were the closest she'd ever come to feeling safe. She trusted him—knew he would jeopardize his own life to protect her.

*Too bad it couldn't last.* When all this was over, Sean would go back to his little girl, and she would go back to her lonely apartment.

Ms. Sophie Brooks, spinster. That was her life. The way it had to be. Even if there were something between her and Sean, she could never tell him everything. He already didn't trust her, didn't want her around Michaela, because he thought she was too much like his ex-wife.

A wry smile twisted her mouth. He had no idea how right he was.

As she stepped into the Weddings Your Way main salon, Vicki, the receptionist, and Julia Garcia, who was showing a client the extensive array of wedding gown accessories, gasped in shock.

"Sophie, what happened to you?" Vicki whispered.

Julia stepped over. "Look at you. Are you all right?"

Sophie nodded.

"If we'd known all it would take to get you out of those skirts and stockings was a fender bender, we could have arranged one a long time ago."

Julia grinned and hugged her.

Sophie awkwardly hugged her back. Another first. No one had ever spontaneously hugged her.

"You look fabulous in that blue," Julia said as her sharp gaze took in the wrist brace and the purple discoloration on her forehead. "Are you sure you're okay?"

Sophie nodded, touching the bruise. "I'm fine. I had a disagreement with an air bag and it won." She smiled tentatively at the two women.

"Oh, Ms. Brennan is waiting to see you and Mr. Majors," Vicki said. "She said to notify her as soon as you got here."

"We'll go on up," Sean said, urging her toward the staircase. His hand still rested protectively on the small of her back.

Sophie glanced back at Julia, who winked and pretended to fan herself. Her message was clear. *Hot guy.*

Sophie just sent her a knowing smile as they started up the staircase.

Rachel Brennan's office door was open, and she was

pacing back and forth, talking on her cell phone. She gestured them in and pointed to the large round table where Rafe Montoya sat.

"That really isn't my problem," she said into the phone. "If you can't do a lineup, get me a photo array. We need to identify this man who has targeted one of my employees."

As Rachel finished her conversation, Rafe looked at Sophie. "How you doing? You look *fantástica* in that blue dress. It's the same color as your eyes."

"Thanks, Rafe. It doesn't quite match my forehead, though, does it?"

"Are you feeling okay? Where have you been all night?" Rafe's black eyes slid over to Sean.

"At Mr. Botero's estate. I spent the night there. Sean thought it would be safest." Sophie didn't mention the kidnappers' call. She figured disclosing that information was Sean's call.

"What did the police find at Sophie's apartment?" Sean asked.

Rafe leaned back and pulled a small notebook from his pocket. "No sign of forced entry. A few fresh scratches on the lock indicate he picked it. He's very good. He relocked your dead bolt from the outside when he left."

"What about the wires?" Sean's voice held a note of impatience.

"Definitely hot." Rafe turned his dark eyes on her. "It's a miracle you weren't electrocuted."

Sean cursed under his breath.

Sophie glanced up and caught a look in his eyes that

she couldn't interpret. He looked angry, but not at her. He looked pale, as if something had scared him.

Thinking about the night before, it was hard for her to believe that she'd been a fraction of a second away from death. "I'd barely stepped into the shower when Sean banged on the door."

Sean nodded, his mouth a thin line, his lips white at the corners.

"What about prints?" Sean asked.

Rafe shook his head. "No prints except for Sophie's—and yours."

Sophie's face grew warm. *How pathetic.* There were no prints because she had no visitors. She rubbed the sore place on her forehead. Her goal had been to depend on no one but herself. She'd apparently succeeded.

"In fact, yours were all over the apartment." Rafe's voice held an accusatory note. "The living room, the refrigerator, her bedside table."

Sean lifted his chin and held Rafe's gaze, his jaw working.

Sophie waited, holding her breath.

Rachel finished her conversation and joined them at the table, breaking the deadlock between the two men. She spared a sharp glance for each of them. As they shifted and lowered their gazes, Rachel spoke to Sophie.

"You need to view a photo array. I'm not sure how much good it will do. The photos will be the employee photos from the hospital, and apparently they never update them. So some will be quite old."

Sophie nodded. "I'll do my best. What will you do if I *can* identify the man I saw? Arrest him?"

"No." Sean's answer was immediate.

Sophie stared at him, as did Rachel and Rafe.

"I believe the man Sophie saw is a major player in this cat-and-mouse game we're in. He identified her and had her followed."

"You think he's in charge?" Rafe muttered.

"It's logical. He got on the elevator on the fourth floor wearing a surgical mask right after Johnson died. He lost her by going through a secured door to the emergency room. Then she left immediately. He must have watched her go to her car. Then either he followed her or, more likely, had someone do it for him."

Rachel nodded briefly. He had her full attention. "Go on," she said.

"He's obviously very good with his hands. He slipped a syringe into Johnson's room and killed him in practically no time. He picked Sophie's double dead bolt lock. He knew how to pull electrical wire."

Rafe scowled. "So why don't you want him picked up?"

"Think about it. If he's involved with Sonya's kidnapping and we pick him up, it will alert the people who may be holding Sonya, and it will put Sophie's life in even more danger."

Rafe nodded reluctantly.

Rachel turned to Sophie. "I think you need to be in a safe house until this is over."

"No, please!" Sophie's heart jumped into her throat. "I need to be here. I need to help."

"There's another issue," Sean interrupted. "Carlos received a phone call this morning." The tension level in the room immediately went up a couple of notches.

"From the kidnappers? Why didn't you say so? What did they say? Do we have a time?"

He shook his head at Rafe. "They refused to give a time. Said they'd be in touch. The ransom has doubled, to four million. They threatened to send Carlos his daughter's thumb to prove how serious they are. And they want him to make the drop."

"Can he do that?" Rachel asked. "He's still very weak, isn't he?"

Sean sat forward. "He'll do it. I'll be there with him."

Rafe doubled his fists on the tabletop. "We still don't know if Sonya is in this country or in Ladera. If the kidnappers are threatening to cut her thumb off and send it to Botero within a reasonable time, it could mean she's still in the U.S."

"It could," Sean agreed, "but it could just be a threat."

"I still don't understand what this has to do with Sophie. Why can't we hide her until this is all over?"

Rafe's voice was harsh. She understood his frustration.

Sean looked intently at Rafe, then at Rachel. "I think Sophie's guy in the mask may be running this operation. He's worried that Sophie can identify him?"

"If he's running it, why did he risk killing Johnson himself? Why not have one of his men do it?"

Sean ticked off the reasons. "We know he has a job at the hospital, because he can enter authorized personnel areas. We know he's arrogant—he likes to handle the big jobs himself. He lets his henchmen do things like following Sophie and me last night. One of his henchmen was keeping me occupied, but I'd bet big money that Sophie's guy was driving the car that forced her off the road. If he thinks he's been fingered, he might disappear on us."

Rachel stood. "In that case, we should spin it to indicate we have no leads."

"Right. But I want Sophie to look at the photos anyway. We can be way ahead if we know who we're looking for. We can check his priors. If we could get hold of his phone records, we might be able to find out who he's in contact with."

"I can take care of that."

Sean's eyes snapped to Rachel's. "Yeah, I've been watching you taking care of things. How does that work exactly, Ms. Wedding Planner Extraordinaire?"

Rafe pushed his chair back, preparing to stand, but Rachel waved a hand.

"That's a fair question, Mr. Majors. Unfortunately I can't answer it just now. Can you trust me when I tell you that I have connections, and I am using them? We are as committed to getting your employer's daughter back safe and sound as you are."

Sean's scalp tightened, and his chest burned with frustration. "I don't like it."

"I'm well aware of that. But I guarantee you that Rafe will keep you fully informed. Now, what are we going to do about Sophie?"

"She stays with me."

Again, all eyes were on him.

"As closely as they've been following her, they have reason to think—" He stopped at a tiny sound from Sophie.

She was blushing and shaking her head at him. But he couldn't worry about her possible embarrassment. His focus was on keeping her alive and safe.

"They have ample reason to think she and I are involved."

Two sets of eyebrows shot up. Sophie's lowered in an embarrassed frown.

"We need to keep them thinking that. Once again, if something changes—if Sophie suddenly disappears— they'll get suspicious."

Rachel folded her arms. "Anything else, Mr. Majors?"

"We need to work out some contingencies. If I'm right, the ransom drop will be tonight. And I'll guarantee you the location won't be anywhere around here."

## Chapter Ten

While Sean and Rafe worked out a plan for backup, Sophie finished up some pending orders for invitations and fended questions from her coworkers.

It was an odd feeling, having people constantly asking how she was doing, whether she needed anything. She found she liked the attention, the feeling that she was part of the group.

From her first memories, she'd always been on the outside looking in. Raised by an Hispanic family, she'd been the odd one out. Growing up so different had been difficult. Her first memories were of being unlike the other children in the neighborhood where she lived.

Eventually, looking different and being treated differently had led to rebellion, which had put her on the path to where she was now. But maybe that could change.

When Julia and Isabelle tentatively approached her with an invitation to have lunch with them, Sophie realized that they had asked her often in the past but she had never said yes before. Eventually they had quit asking.

This time, she smiled and accepted, and cringed when they looked surprised.

Lunch with them was the most fun she'd had in a long time.

No one talked about the case, or her injuries. Instead, they talked about fashion, food, yoga, movies—girl things.

When they got back to Weddings Your Way, Sean was pacing.

Sophie thanked Julia and Isabelle for asking her to lunch and walked past Sean to her desk.

He followed.

"Where have you been?" His eyes held the promise of a thunderstorm.

She sat down and looked up at him. "We went to lunch."

He pushed his suit jacket back and stuck his hands in his pockets. "Didn't we just agree that you would stay with me?"

She was still exhilarated from the carefree lunch and in a playful mood. She widened her eyes. "Oh, did you mean 24/7? I must have missed that part."

He scowled. "What you apparently missed is the fact that your life is in danger. I guess you're still searching for that bigger thrill."

She cringed at the censure in his expression.

"I'm sorry. I really didn't think lunch with two other—" She stopped. She'd almost said *two other Confidential agents.* "Two other people would be a problem," she finished.

Sean took his hands out of his pockets and straightened his suit jacket. "The photos are here. You need to view them."

Sophie stood. "Of course. Where are they?"

"Upstairs, in Rachel's office. They were just delivered."

It only took a few minutes with a magnifying glass to identify the man she'd ridden in the elevator with. "It's him. I'm certain. See that scar? It cuts through his right eyebrow."

Sean sat on one side of her and Rafe sat on the other.

"You're absolutely certain?" Sean asked.

Sophie looked at the photo again. "I recognize the look in his eyes, too." She shuddered.

Sean took the photos and stacked them, while Rafe pulled another folder toward them.

"Okay, Soph," Rafe said. "Now comes the hard part." He spread out a dozen or so photographs, most of them small, and every single one of the subjects had a scar on the right side of his forehead.

She stared at the array. "You've got to be kidding me. Where did all these come from?"

Sean put a hand on her shoulder. "It's a photo lineup. We can't take any chances."

His hand was warm. She longed to lay her cheek against it, to soak up his strength and concern. But he squeezed her shoulder lightly and took his hand away.

She drew in a deep breath. "So you mean all but one of these guys are ringers, like in a regular lineup. Okay. Let me have the magnifying glass." Her hand shook as she held it over each photo in turn. What if she couldn't identify him? She didn't have to ask that question; she knew the answer. She had to make the proper ID. They were counting on her to give them a starting point.

With her ID, they could check his identification papers, his phone records, recent purchases, any trips he'd made.

While she looked at picture after picture, Sean's cell phone rang.

"What? When?" His voice took on a strained quality. He glanced at Sophie and Rafe, then walked out into the hallway.

Sophie and Rafe exchanged a glance. She knew that Rafe was thinking the same thing she was. What if it was the kidnappers? She looked toward the door.

"We'll know soon enough," Rafe said. "Right now, you need to concentrate on the photos."

She did. So far none of them looked like the guy she'd spent a few seconds in the elevator with. One's scar was too high. Another one's hair was too light. Another photo looked as if it had been retouched to give the appearance of a scar. Then she saw him. The man in the surgical mask.

"This is him," she said, tapping the last photo. She picked it up and held it close under the magnifying glass. "It's him. I know it."

Rafe leaned over and kissed her on the cheek. "Good going, Soph. Now I've got to get the paperwork started so we can get his information."

She sat back in her chair, shaking. "Thank goodness. I was really worried when I saw all those pictures of men with scars on their foreheads."

Sean returned, pocketing his cell phone. A muscle twitched in his jaw.

"Sean? What's wrong? Has Mr. Botero heard from the kidnappers?"

He shook his head. "No. Nothing like that. We need to go. Now."

"Majors?" Rafe stood.

Sean's even gaze met Rafe's. "The call was personal."

Rafe eyed him for a moment, then nodded.

Sean turned to Sophie. "We need to go."

"Sophie can stay here," Rafe said. "I'll be around all afternoon."

Sean shook his head.

His demeanor worried Sophie. She stood. "Has something happened to Michaela? To Rosita?"

Placing his hand at the small of her back, Sean silently guided her out of Rachel's office and toward the stairs.

"Sean? Are you still angry with me for going to lunch? Is that what this is about? I've apologized. I'll stick to your side like glue from now on."

Her words only deepened his scowl.

"Are you going to take me back to my apartment?"

"I wish. Your apartment is a crime scene." His voice was gruff.

"Oh." She should have realized that. For the moment she was homeless, and her only clothes were at Botero's estate. "That puts me in a rather difficult position. I don't have any clothes."

As they passed the receptionist's desk, Vicki held out a fancy pink-and-white bag to Sean with a flirtatious smile. Sean ignored the smile, took the bag, and handed it to Sophie. "Yes, you do. Rachel took care of it. She sent Vicki out while you were having your two-hour lunch."

Irritated, she stopped. He was stubborn as a mule. "Do you think you'll be over that any time in—say—the next five years?"

He sent her a scathing look and walked out into the Miami heat. Clouds were building out over the ocean.

"If you need to take care of a personal problem, why don't I stay here? I'll be safe. There's no reason you have to babysit me."

He rounded on her. "There's nothing I'd like better than to let you stay here with your top-secret buddies. But I can't. I don't want to trust your safety to anyone else. I need you alive."

Sophie suffered his intense stare. "So you're arrogant, too, like the man in the surgical mask. You think you're the only one who can do the job."

His frown grew deeper. "If that's how you want to look at it. I call it being prepared. It's my boss's daughter who's missing, and you hold the only clue to the identity of her kidnappers."

He clicked the remote lock on his car and climbed in. She got in on the passenger side. As she settled into the seat, he continued, "Every time I let you out of my sight, you get into trouble."

"So where are we going?"

"There's something I have to do."

After a few abortive attempts to start a conversation, Sophie closed her eyes and let the warm Miami sun shine on her sore forehead.

She sat up when a right turn took the car into darkness.

"So you finally decided to wake up?"

"I wasn't asleep. Where are we?" Sophie squinted, waiting for her eyes to dark-adapt.

"At my apartment."

"Oh, no. Why would you bring me back here?" He didn't want her at his home, near his daughter. What was he doing?

They got out of the car and stepped into the elevator.

"That was Rosita on the phone. One of her grandchildren broke his leg."

So he had no choice. He had to bring her here.

"Is he okay?"

Sean nodded as he unlocked his apartment and stood back for her to enter. "I don't think it's serious. But she wants to check on him."

Sophie started to answer when a tiny blond whirlwind blew into the room.

"Dad-dee!"

Sean's face softened into a beautiful smile and he knelt in time for Michaela to throw herself into his arms. He stood, hugging her and receiving a big smacking kiss.

Sophie took a step backward, retreating from the painfully sweet moment between father and daughter. She blinked at a ridiculous stinging at the back of her eyes.

"Daddy. How did you come home so quick? You're way early!"

"I came to see my little sprout. Have you seen my sprout?" He kissed her forehead.

Michaela jabbed her thumb into her chest. "That's me. I'm your little sprout."

He laughed and hugged her again. "That's right! I forgot."

Looking at the two of them hurt Sophie in a deep, hidden place. And yet at the same time, it was poignant and uplifting. She felt like crying and laughing at the same time. She also felt she was intruding.

As she took another step backward, Michaela's green eyes landed on her.

"Daddy! It's Soph-ee. You brought Sophie." She wriggled around in his arms and reached out toward Sophie.

"Sophie. You came to see me!"

Sean held on to her as she strained toward Sophie. He raised his brows. "Aren't you going to take her?"

"I—" How could she tell him or his daughter that she knew nothing about children? That they frightened and saddened her, that she'd rather be caught in a crossfire than have to deal with a toddler.

"Sophie… Daddy, I want Sophie to hold me." Michaela's voice threatened tears.

"Okay. Here we go," Sophie said tightly, holding out her arms and staggering a bit as Michaela threw all her weight at her.

She wrapped her arms around the sturdy little body. *Oh, she felt good.* Warm and alive and full of energy. She smelled fresh and new with a hint of bubblegum, and her hair was as soft as angel's hair. Tears clogged the back of Sophie's throat. At that moment if she tried to talk, she'd burst into tears. So she just hugged Michaela.

"Ah, finally!" It was Rosita. She was carrying her purse. "Now I won't be gone very long. I just need to see that little Joaquin is all right. Good afternoon, Miss Sophie."

"Hi, Rosita." Sophie was surprised at the warmth with which Rosita greeted her. "I hope your grandson is all right."

"Ack, that *muchacho*. He will be fine. But *su abuela* must be there." Rosita beamed.

*"La abuela sabe la mejor medicina,"* Sophie said.

Rosita chuckled. *"Y usted es muy inteligente."*

After Rosita left, Sean reached for Michaela. "What was that all about?"

"You don't speak Spanish?"

He shrugged. "I got 'grandmother' and 'medicine' and 'very smart.'"

"I just said, 'Grandmothers have the best medicine.'"

For a minute, Sean looked at her oddly. "Rosita always referred to herself as my grandmamma. She used to tell me that."

Sophie smiled.

"Come on, sprout," he said, reaching for Michaela. "I'm sure Miss Sophie is tired of holding you."

Michaela's hands tightened around Sophie's neck. "No. Sophie, play my game with me."

"Michaela," Sophie said, "I think your daddy wants you to go with him."

He held up his hands. "Oh, no. I've played her game, for hours. You deserve to have that pleasure. While you and Michaela are playing, I'm going to take a shower, then you can bathe and change if you want to."

Sophie stared at his smile as his little girl clung to her neck. She was surrounded with everything she'd ever wanted, and none of it was hers. She knew she was secretly poaching these loving moments from Sean, but he had so much love—from Michaela, from Rosita—he wouldn't miss the tiny bit she stole for herself. It would end soon enough.

WHEN SEAN CAME out of the shower a half hour later, shirtless and buttoning the top button of his jeans, he stuck his head into the living room to see how Sophie was faring with his daughter, who on her best behavior was a constant bundle of never-ending energy.

The sight that greeted him put a crack in the brittle shell that housed his heart. Sophie was curled up on his leather couch with Michaela cradled in her arms, asleep.

It had worried him that his little sprout had taken to Sophie so quickly and trustingly. Michaela was rarely wrong about people. She either loved them or shied away completely. He'd fully expected her not to like Sophie, so the fact that she'd asked about her every day had surprised and disturbed him.

Right now, she lay in Sophie's arms, her little face composed and trusting, limp with sleep.

Sean raised his gaze to Sophie's. She rested her head on top of Michaela's, and her eyes were closed.

He stepped closer. Her eyes were something else, too. He took another step.

Her eyes were wet. She'd been crying. An unfamiliar ache started in his chest. He had the urge to wipe her tears away. No. He wanted to *kiss* them away. His jaw tensed as his brain quickly moved from a stray thought of a tender, platonic kiss to the uninhibited passion they'd shared in his bed.

His arousal sprung to life, chafing against the tight denim of his jeans.

*She's too much like Cindy,* he reminded himself, but even that didn't help. This was only the second time Sophie had met Michaela, and she was already sharing with her a moment more tender than Michaela's mother ever had.

He shifted from one foot to the other, trying to suppress his desire for her, but even thoughts of his ex-wife didn't distract him from Sophie's delicate features, her unconscious grace and sexiness.

She opened her eyes. For a long moment they stared at each other. Sean had no idea what she was feeling, but his brain wouldn't let go of the vision of her lying on her stomach, naked to his view, as he did his best to kiss away the pain of each of the small, cruel scars that marred her lovely body.

"Do you want to put her to bed?" Sophie's voice was barely audible.

He nodded, but he didn't move for a few seconds, until he regained control of his body. From the blush that rose in Sophie's cheeks, she saw his struggle.

As he crossed the room, her gaze slid down from his face, across his bare chest and down.

He groaned low in his throat.

"I see what you mean about her game," Sophie whispered as he lifted his sleeping daughter from her embrace. "You could have warned me that it consisted of her running across the room and jumping into my lap over and over and over again."

Sean grinned at her as he cradled Michaela. "And deny you the pleasure of finding out for yourself? Never."

She smiled back at him, a genuine, unguarded smile, and he nearly gasped to see her exquisite beauty.

"Go ahead," he said, nodding toward the bathroom. "The shower is all yours. Use the one in my bedroom. I'll put Michaela in her bed."

Sophie stood. She put out her hand to pat Michaela's back as she passed.

Sean looked down at her. As if she felt his gaze, she raised her face to his and he saw the traces of tears on her cheeks.

"Why were you crying?" he murmured.

Sophie shook her head. "She's just so perfect. So beautiful." Her voice broke. She pressed her lips together.

At that moment, Sean realized that whatever Sophie was hiding, it had to do with a child. He didn't know if it was lingering fear and distrust because of her own childhood, or if it was something more recent. But the tightly controlled, carefully hidden sadness behind her eyes stirred him in a totally different, non-physical way.

Clutching his baby tightly to him, he acknowledged for the first time just how desperately he wanted to know more about Sophie Brooks. He wanted to know her thoughts, her fears, her desires.

"Sophie?" His lips formed her name almost sound-lessly.

A flicker of fear brightened her eyes for an instant, then she dropped her gaze to his lips.

Leaning down, he kissed her softly on the mouth. She parted her lips and sighed. Still holding Michaela, Sean bent and deepened the kiss.

They weren't touching at all, except for their lips, but Sean felt her against him, inside him, covering him. For that moment, their souls were entwined.

The innocent contact of their mouths was more inti-mate than anything he'd ever done, because it was not only physical contact, but emotional.

Sophie stopped it. She pulled away and ducked her head. "I'd better shower," she said, glancing around for the pink-and-white shopping bag. Spotting it, she grabbed it and practically ran from the room.

Sean stood still, his hand absently rubbing Mi-chaela's back, and relived those last few seconds before Sophie made her escape.

She'd felt it, too. He was certain. As little as he knew about her, as suspicious as he was of her motives, he knew one thing. She wanted him. She craved his touch as much as he craved hers.

And just like him, she was fighting it with all her strength.

BY THE TIME Sophie got out of the shower and dressed in the beautiful silk underwear and tasteful beige linen pants and sleeveless top Vicki had bought for her, Rosita was back and Sean was dressed and pacing.

He looked up when she entered the living room, a spark of appreciation showing in his eyes. "Good. You're ready."

"This is going to be a bad night, I can already tell," Rosita was saying. "You have let Michaela sleep for hours. She will be awake all night."

"Let her sleep until we're gone," he said, pointing a finger to reinforce his point. "Then tell her Daddy will be back in the morning. She had a busy afternoon, jumping on Sophie."

Rosita's black eyes snapped to Sophie, and she nodded. *"Bueno."*

Before Sophie could wonder about that curt comment, Sean glanced at his watch and gestured for Sophie. "Come on. I need to get to Carlos's. It's been too long. I need to check in with my men, and make sure Carlos is okay."

"I could stay here with Rosita and Michaela—"

"No," he snapped. "I told you. You stay with me."

Sophie met Rosita's gaze and saw a look on the woman's face that appeared to be satisfaction. She raised her eyebrows at her.

Sean shrugged into his suit jacket and held out his arm. Sophie let him guide her out the door and down the elevator to his car.

He made record time getting to Carlos's estate. At the gate, he questioned the guard and found out that nothing unusual had happened, but before they drove the few dozen feet to the house, his cell phone rang.

"Patch them through, now!"

It was the kidnappers! Sophie's heart stuck in her throat. Sean yanked the keys out of the ignition and shot out of the car, sprinting across the driveway and into the house, leaving Sophie to catch up.

By the time she got to Botero's study, Sean was listening in on the phone call and directing Carlos in what to say.

The old man looked frailer than the last time Sophie had seen him. The uncertainty over his daughter's safety was taking its toll.

"I need to know my daughter is safe," he said, his voice thready with weakness and emotion.

Sean's eyes were like storm clouds as he listened to the answer. He shook his head at Botero.

The older man nodded his understanding. He took a shaky breath. "No! I will not cooperate unless you can prove to me that my Sonya is alive."

Javier, Carlos's nurse, had a hand on his wrist, taking his pulse and looking worried.

Sophie clasped her hands, hardly breathing.

"That is not good enough. You must let me hear my daughter or you can go to hell." Carlos's frail hand dropped the phone into its cradle.

Sean let out a long breath. "I'm not sure that was a good idea, Mr. Botero," he said carefully.

Sophie could see the restrained tension in the set of his shoulders. He wasn't sure what the kidnappers would do.

Carlos's dark eyes met his security chief's gaze. "I know what I am doing, Sean. They will call back." He nodded. "They will put her on the phone, or they will not get a penny, and they know that."

Javier looked up. "I need to give Mr. Botero his medication."

Sean nodded. "Come on, Sophie. Let's go get some coffee."

Outside the door of the study, she confronted him. "You don't think Sonya is still alive, do you?"

Sean rubbed his face. "I don't know. It all depends on what the kidnappers' ultimate purpose is. If they need money, then we're in good shape, and Sonya is probably fine. If they have no agenda other than to keep Juan DeLeon's mind off the upcoming legislative session, it's a toss-up."

"If it's DeLeon they're concerned about, why are they sending the ransom demands to Mr. Botero?"

"That's a good question. My theory is that by targeting Carlos instead of DeLeon, they could keep the focus here in the U.S. DeLeon can easily travel between the two countries. Botero can't."

Sophie watched the play of emotions on Sean's face. "You care a great deal about Mr. Botero, don't you?"

"I've worked for him for ten years. He trusts me. He believes I can do anything." Sean shook his head and rubbed the back of his neck.

"Well, you can, can't you?"

He glanced up and she smiled.

His features softened. "You made quite an impression on Michaela," he said.

His change of subject surprised her, and to her chagrin, her eyes stung with tears. "She is so wonderful."

"Why were you really crying?"

Her pulse hammered. "I told you," she muttered, evading his gaze.

"Sophie?"

Looking beyond him, she bit her lip, then sighed. "I'm sorry, Sean. I didn't mean to let her see, but she was running and jumping, and she saw the scar on my shoulder." Her hand went to the raised ridge that was barely covered by the sleeveless top. "And she—" Her voice broke.

She swallowed and took a deep breath, trying to calm her racing pulse. She looked down. "She asked me who hurt me, and—"

Sean's hand touched her chin.

Against her will, she raised her gaze to him and felt a tear fall.

"—and she kissed it."

Sean's eyes were deep teal. He grazed his fingertips over the corner of her mouth and up to caress her cheek. His thumb wiped away the tear. "My daughter is very softhearted."

*Like you.* Despite her resolve never to think about the one night they'd shared, Sophie's brain fed her a memory of his careful, soothing kisses on each of her scars. Then on top of that came the erotic image of him above her, his soft blue gaze holding hers as he brought her to a pinnacle of sensation she'd never before experienced.

She felt another tear gather and fall.

Sean's cell phone rang.

*The kidnappers.*

He whirled and headed back into the study.

Sophie wiped her eyes and followed.

Carlos looked a little better. A half-empty glass of water sat at his elbow. His skeletal fingers picked up the phone.

Sean pressed his Receive button at the same time.

Sophie waited, her hands tented at her mouth.

Carlos's face crumpled. "Sonya! *Mi corazón! ¿Cómo estás?* Have they hurt you?"

As Sean listened to the small, frightened voice of Sonya Botero, his jaw ached with tension and his fingers tightened around his cell phone.

"*Papá,*" she said. "I am all right. Very hungry. I want a pizza—"

"Enough!" the gruff voice Sean had heard on the last phone call interrupted her.

"Sonya! Sonya?" The stereo anguish of Carlos's voice on the phone and in person echoed in Sean's ears.

*Damn it!* The bastards.

"There, old man. Now you've heard your daughter."

Carlos put a shaky hand over his eyes. "*Sí.* I heard her." He let loose a string of curses in Spanish. Out of the corner of his eye, Sean saw Sophie's face turn red.

Sean walked over and put his hand on Carlos's shoulder and squeezed. He needed to remain calm. Sean didn't want anything to get in the way of this meeting. He bit his tongue to keep from asking where Sonya was. From the sound of the phone connection, he didn't think she was in the same place as the kidnapper.

Sean had the definite impression that Sonya was not in the U.S. He feared she was in Ladera, which meant all the kidnappers wanted was Carlos's money. His boss wouldn't see his daughter. Not today.

Carlos gave Sean a brief nod and stopped his tirade. "What do you want?" he asked tiredly.

"You try our patience, old man. Do you have the four million U.S. dollars?"

Sean nodded at Carlos.

"Of course. I keep my word."

"Then we will meet in two hours."

"Where?" Carlos's hands were shaking badly.

Sean grabbed a pen as the kidnapper spoke.

"There is a vacant warehouse down near the docks off West Street. The freight door will be open. Drive inside and wait. Come alone."

Sean touched Carlos's shoulder and shook his head. They'd discussed this. He hoped Carlos didn't forget to tell the kidnappers he had to have a driver, that he couldn't drive himself.

"I am disabled. I cannot walk or drive. My chauffeur will be driving. I will be in the backseat with your money."

"You're lying! No driver. We will kill your daughter."

Carlos sat up straight. His drawn face drained of color. "*Señor,* I do not lie. All I care about is my daughter."

Sean's heart went out to him. He held the phone so tightly Sean thought the plastic might break. "You will meet with me and my driver, or we will not meet at all. It is the only way you will get the money."

After a pause, the voice said, "Fine. You and your driver. No one else."

Sean hadn't heard a word exchanged during that pause. It was just for effect. Was this Sophie's masked man?

"You have my word. There will only be two of us."

"Two hours. Four million dollars. If anything goes wrong, that instant will be your daughter's last breath."

"You will bring her—?"

The phone went dead.

## Chapter Eleven

Sophie rode with Sean to pick up the four million dollars. They went in the limousine so the bank employees could load the two large cases into the trunk.

Sophie stood beside Sean as two burly guards rolled a cart carrying the metal cases to the back of the limo and hefted them into the trunk.

"Mr. Botero looked really drained after the phone call. He can't possibly do this," Sophie said.

Sean shook his head. "He won't. Javier is giving him a sedative. One of my men is an expert shot. He's ready to go. He'll wear Carlos's coat and hat and sit in the back. I'll pick him up when I take you back to the estate."

Sophie had already noticed the dark coat and hat in the backseat of the limo. "Won't a coat and hat in the middle of summer be suspicious?"

He shook his head. "Since his stroke, Carlos hasn't gone anywhere without them. You know his reputation. He's nearly as popular in the Hispanic community as his daughter Sonya. Well-known in Miami society. He's a proud man. Doesn't want to be seen as weak and frail. So even when he goes to the doctor, he wears those."

The bank employees finally wrestled the second suitcase into the limo and signaled to Sean that he was set to go.

"Do you think they'll have Sonya there?"

Sean didn't answer, but his jaw worked as he stepped to the back of the car to check the suitcases and close the trunk. Then he came around to open the passenger door for her. As he reached for the handle, his cell phone rang.

He answered it.

Sophie couldn't tell what the voice was saying, but Sean's face turned white.

Sophie grabbed his forearm. The muscle under her hand jumped, but he didn't look at her.

"When? Just now? How is he?" He cursed. "Call an ambulance. No sirens. Just get him to the hospital."

He listened for a couple of seconds. "Good. So they're on their way. You tell him I'll take care of this."

He snapped his phone shut and slammed his other palm against the column next to which they'd parked.

"Sean, what's wrong?"

He sent her a quelling glance as color began to return to his face. He looked at his watch and cursed again. "The kidnappers called again. They've moved the time up. One hour."

"Of course. We should have expected that."

He frowned. "What?"

"Never mind. What about the ambulance? Is Carlos okay?"

"He had a stroke, right after he hung up." Sean's face reflected his worry. "Javier says it wasn't major, but he's lost all strength on the left side of his body. He can't make the ransom drop. Hell, there's no time now, even if he could. Dear God, they'll kill Sonya!"

Sophie remembered Carlos's coat and hat. "I'll do it."

Sean's eyes turned lethal. "The hell you will."

"They said one hour? How much time do we have left? Can we get to that warehouse in time?"

"Not even in a jet. We only have ten minutes. Forget it, Sophie. I'll go alone." He ran a hand down his face in frustration.

"That won't work. Mr. Botero is stooped and frail now. I'll wear his coat and hat and huddle in the backseat."

Sean grabbed her elbow, not gently. "Are you pulling that 'I love danger' crap again? I'm warning you, Sophie, this is not the time."

She laid her hand over his. "Listen to me. I can do this. I am an agent of a discreet, covert division of the Department of Public Safety. It's known as the Confidential Agency. Weddings Your Way is a cover for the operation."

Sean's head jerked as if he'd been hit. He gaped at her. "Have you gone nuts? What the hell are you talking about?"

"You have to trust me. I'm trained for this sort of thing. Before I became a Confidential agent, I worked with the CIA in New York."

He slammed his palm on the limo's roof. "Damn it, don't screw with me! This is life and death, not some—"

"Sean!" she interrupted sharply. "I can't prove it to you now, but if we're going to save Sonya's life, you have to believe me. We've got to go."

Sean stared at the tall, lovely blonde, trying to absorb what she was saying. He couldn't. He'd heard the words. Some of them had even made sense. Like *Confidential agent. Weddings Your Way is a cover. CIA.* But coming out of her mouth they were impossible to believe.

She returned his gaze without blinking, her chin lifted in that determined way he was beginning to recognize.

He had no choice. There was too much at stake. Sonya's life. And Carlos's, because Sean knew beyond a shadow of a doubt that if Sonya died, Carlos would die, too.

And he was responsible. He couldn't let that happen.

He'd do what he had to do to protect his boss and his boss's daughter, even believe an unbelievable story from a woman he'd only known a short time, and couldn't afford to trust.

He studied Sophie's face for a precious few seconds. "Get in."

Sophie's cheeks ballooned in a huge whooshing breath of relief. She knew Sean didn't believe her. But that was of secondary importance. He'd figured out that he had no choice but to go along with her plan.

She'd worry about what he did and didn't believe later. She'd deal with the consequences once they were out of danger.

She climbed into the backseat of the limousine and wriggled into the coat.

"Do you have a gun?" she asked, pushing up the brim of the hat enough to see as he started the limo and pulled out of the bank's covered parking area.

"A gun?" His gaze met hers in the rear view mirror.

"Yes, Sean, a gun. We're going to meet dangerous men in a deserted warehouse. I think we both should be armed."

"But your wrist is sprained."

She sent him a wry smile. "I can shoot with either hand." She felt sorry for him. He looked stunned. He was a victim of TMI—too much information in too little time.

"Look in the armrest," he finally said.

She pulled down the retractable armrest and opened it.

"Nice," she commented as she pulled a 9 mm from the storage compartment. Deftly, she expelled the magazine, checked it and slapped it back into the gun, all the time feeling Sean's eyes on her.

"How far are we from the warehouse?"

"About three miles." He frowned, then took out his cell phone. "I'm calling Montoya. We need backup."

"Tell him I've told you about Confidential. He'll position police outside the warehouse. But the kidnappers will probably have lookouts, too. Warn him."

Sean had already dialed the number. "Montoya. The ransom's going down right now. Nope, no time. Sophie told me about Confidential. Can you get us some backup to 2497 West Street? Yep. Empty warehouse."

He listened. "Who knows. Probably surrounded. Just Sophie and me. Carlos had another stroke. Hell, man, we've got less than ten minutes. We're already late. Get that backup and keep it outside. We're in Botero's limo. Don't let them do anything unless they hear shots. Otherwise wait for my call. I don't want to lose these guys. Yes, I'll take care of Sophie."

Sean closed his cell phone and turned onto the street the warehouse was on. *Take care of Sophie.* It sounded like Sophie could take care of herself.

He didn't have time to consider how he felt about her and everyone else at that damned wedding planning place lying to him. He'd known from the start that there was something fishy about the whole operation.

A division of the Department of Public Safety. That was vague enough. Who knew what it meant.

He glanced in the rearview mirror at Sophie. She looked small and vulnerable in Carlos's coat and hat. The sleeve of the coat hid her weapon.

Her gaze met his and she smiled tightly and nodded, her blue eyes sharp and determined.

In that instant, he saw her differently. She was a professional, a trained agent. Gone was any trace of the ditzy blonde who craved excitement and danger.

The image of her slapping at her back where a paddle holster would rest, then ducking and rolling flashed through his mind. Watching her check and load that gun just now had been a huge turn-on.

*Hell.* Down, boy. This was no time to get hot and bothered about his mysterious partner.

"Here it is," he said, turning into the short driveway of the warehouse. The freight door was open just enough to clear the top of the limousine.

They drove into darkness.

The limo's lights switched on automatically, along with a couple of recessed lights inside the vehicle that emitted a soft, eerie glow. Sean lowered the car windows.

"Can you see anything?" Sophie whispered. The late afternoon light from the open freight door sent long shadows snaking across the concrete floor and into the hidden corners. Above them, a skeletal framework of rafters provided dozens of hiding places for lookouts and sharpshooters.

Sean shook his head. His hair brushed the collar of his jacket, nearly hiding his vulnerable nape and planting a soft yearning in Sophie's breast. She'd kissed him there, had pressed her nose into his hair and breathed him in—the faint scent of woodsy shampoo, the warm musk of his freshly washed skin, the sharp redolence of citrus mouthwash.

The sound of metal raking metal startled her, destroying the poignant memory of their one night together.

Sean shifted in his seat and Sophie realized he was checking his weapon. The sound had been the snick of a full magazine snapping into place.

"So what the hell were you talking about back there?" His soft yet harsh voice reproached her.

"Rachel Brennan is the head of the Miami Confidential Agency. We work with the Department of Public Safety on certain matters that require discretion."

Sean laughed shortly. "Discretion. Is that what you call it?"

There was a mountain of recrimination in his words. She bit her lip as she watched the line of his jaw bulge

as he quickly and with no wasted effort checked out the
area around the car.

"I didn't mean to lie to you."

"And yet you did."

"I follow Rachel's orders." She winced. That comment was going to open up a can of worms.

"Yeah?" He turned his head. His classic profile made
her heart flutter. His furrowed brows and set mouth
made it ache. He disliked her and she was just about to
find out how much.

"Just how far does a 'Confidential agent' go to
follow orders?"

"Sean, I know what you must think—"

"I doubt it."

She swallowed and squeezed her eyes shut for an
instant. Then she took a deep breath and did something
she thought she would never do again in her life. She
took down all the barriers. With her pulse hammering
and her chest tight, she told him the truth.

"Not that night, Sean."

He didn't even blink.

She put her hand over her mouth to stifle a sob. *Stop
it, Sophie,* she admonished herself. Think about the job.

She surveyed the warehouse interior again. It was
easier this time. Her eyes were adapting to the dark. But
she still didn't see anything move.

"What about the scars, Sophie? I guess you lied
about those, too. What really happened? Something in
the line of duty?"

She clenched her teeth as she hefted her weapon in
her left hand and searched the rafters for any sign of
movement. "I didn't lie," she said tightly.

"I grant I'm not a good judge of women." His voice grated. "I tend to believe in them until I'm proven wrong. I believed in my wife, until she told me herself that she'd cheated on me throughout our whole marriage. Including when she got pregnant."

Her eyes prickled with tears. "Sean—"

"I even believed Michaela was my daugh—" He stopped.

"Oh, no! Sean. Your wife told you Michaela wasn't yours? That's too cruel. It can't be true! She has your eyes. Your jaw. That stubborn glare."

Sean's head bent slightly, then lifted again. He turned his head to survey the area on his left. "I asked you a question."

She swallowed. She'd already flayed herself raw. What did the rest of it matter? "What really happened? You want the whole sad story?"

"Got nothing else to do right now."

Sophie let her tear-hazed gaze roam around the deserted warehouse. "Okay. Try to keep up, because I've never told this before and I'm only going to tell it once." She took a long breath.

"I was found only a few hours old, at the door of a Catholic church. No one had any idea who I was or who had left me there. The cleaning lady, Lourdes Ruiz, had just had a baby, so she took me home. I called her Mama. But I was difficult—different. And Mama was very strict. When I was seventeen I ran away. I thought my boyfriend was the greatest guy in the world. I did crack, got pregnant, lost my baby and my boyfriend on the same day. When I recovered, I decided to learn how to take care of myself. And here I am."

She was amazed that she'd gotten through the whole thing without breaking. She'd kept her voice even, unemotional, just like she'd hoped she could.

Somehow, the fact that he wasn't looking at her made it harder, not easier. His profile had softened as she'd talked. His jaw had unclenched. His brows were no longer pulled down in a frown.

Sobs were crowding the back of her throat, but she'd be damned if she'd cry in front of him. She held her breath.

He turned his head slightly toward her and a faint, wet glimmer lit his eyes.

*Don't,* she wanted to shout. *Don't pity me.*

"So all those scars are from beatings your adoptive mother gave you?"

She couldn't say anything else. It was too much. She'd given Sean more than she'd ever given anyone in her life. And he'd given her more in return.

But she couldn't give it all. It was too humiliating, too painful.

"Sophie? You're still lying."

She grimaced. Where were the damn kidnappers? She'd welcome a shoot-out right now.

Blowing out an audible breath, she surrendered. "Okay. You want the entire pathetic story of poor Sophie? You want to feel superior and self-righteous because you forced me to give up all my secrets? Fine." Anger felt good. It cleansed and energized. She let it flow over her, let it build.

"You want even more proof that I'm not fit to be around you or your daughter? Well, you're in luck today, because you've got it. You think I don't know that you've hated every moment Michaela was *exposed* to me? You think I don't know she—you—both of you are way too good for me?"

"Sophie, don't—"

"Well I do know it. I didn't want to get involved with you. I begged you not to touch me. I didn't want to meet Michaela, or play with her, or hold her. I don't do babies and families. My life was perfectly fine before you came into it, and it will be perfectly fine again. I know who I am and where I came from."

Her hand was cramping around the gun. She set it down in her lap and flexed her fingers, then picked it up again.

"No. All the scars are not from Mama. The bad ones—including the one on my shoulder—are courtesy of my baby's father. Courtesy of his gang's specially crafted gold belt buckle. Let's say he wasn't happy that I let myself get pregnant."

"Ah, Sophie…"

"No!" She slapped the butt of the gun against the car's armrest. "Do *not* pity me. You got what you wanted, but you have no right to sit in your ivory tower with your beautiful baby and your perfect life and pity me."

"I wasn't—"

With the suddenness of a gunshot, the lights came on.

Sophie jerked. Sean went totally still. Without moving another muscle, Sophie flipped the safety off her gun with her thumb. The click sounded loud in the brilliant silence. She reached up and pushed the brim of Botero's hat up her forehead.

"Careful, *Mr. Botero,*" Sean whispered loudly, reminding her of her role.

She slouched down in the seat, clutching her gun. She'd shot weapons one-handed, even left-handed, during her training with the CIA, but she knew her sprained wrist was going to hamper her.

Sean's cell phone jangled. He muttered a curse as he flipped the phone open.

Sophie forced herself to breathe long and slow. Her gaze darted around the bare, musty building. She saw nothing. No movement. Where were they?

"Yeah?" Sean grunted.

Sophie carefully folded the sleeve of Carlos Botero's coat up her forearm. She needed to be ready.

"This is his chauffeur," Sean said gruffly. "He has instructed me to speak for him. He asked me to tell you he's tired and ready to get this over with."

He paused, listening, then turned his head, his intense teal gaze meeting hers.

"Mr. Botero. I am to tell you *un arma está apuntada a su cabeza.*"

Sophie nodded briefly. Sean bungled the pronunciation, but the words were clear enough. *There is a gun aimed at your head.*

Sean needed to know what they'd said.

She spoke in a guttural whisper. Who knew how close they were? "Tell them I am not impressed with their theatrics. They will speak English. And I do not care about guns aimed at my head. I only care about my daughter."

Sean's eyes turned stormy and he stiffened.

Sophie shook her head infinitesimally. *Don't worry about me.* She lifted her gun's barrel slightly.

His gaze dipped, he scowled, but he repeated her words to the caller. He continued to watch her as he listened.

"No. Not yet. You show yourselves. Have the *cojones* to face the man whose daughter you're holding against her will."

Sophie darted a glance around her.

The sound of Sean's cell phone snapping shut grated on her already frayed nerves. "What did they say?"

"Nothing. They hung up." He unhooked his seat belt. "I'm getting out."

"No, Sean. You'll be a perfect target." Sophie released her own belt.

"I told them to show themselves. I need to do the same. Just stay still and be ready." He searched her face. "Swear to me you're telling the truth and you know how to use that gun."

She held his gaze. "I swear. I won't let you down. I won't let Michaela down."

He blinked, then turned around and got out of the car, pulling his chauffeur's cap down to shadow his face.

As he did, Sophie saw movement from the far side of the warehouse. A medium-height Hispanic man dressed in black swaggered toward them. Behind him, two other men appeared. All three were armed.

Sophie adjusted her grip on her weapon. She could take them all out once they got about twenty feet closer, but not before at least one of them had time to shoot. She'd take out the front man first.

As he drew closer, she saw a prominent scar above his brow. It was her masked man. He was obviously the leader.

Every muscle in her body twitched to turn and see if Sean had recognized him, but she couldn't let down her guard even for an instant. Her job was to cover him.

From behind her and to her right, she heard the snick of a rifle being cocked. It was the sharpshooter the caller had promised. She felt the shooter's line of sight like a laser beam aimed at her right temple.

"Stop right there." Sean's voice was harsh, authoritative, controlled.

The leader smiled and deliberately walked several paces closer. "So Señor Botero lets his driver give the orders? Where are his *cojones?*" The man angled his head and peered at Sophie. "Eh, old man? Perhaps you lost them when you lost your daughter. We were distressed to hear that you have been ill. We will make this quick and painless."

Suddenly, he kicked the right front fender of the limousine. "Get out of the car, old man. Show us your face."

Sean almost fired his gun when the man moved. He was jumpy as a cat. The idea that it was Sophie sitting there in the car, hampered by the oversized coat and hat and her sprained wrist made him crazy.

If he already had his gun in hand, he could take out all three men, but since it was in his pocket, he wouldn't get more than two before they shot him.

He could probably count on Sophie for one, but he

didn't want to bank on it. Plus, he'd heard a noise behind him. Maybe the promised sharpshooter with a rifle aimed at Sophie's head. Who knew how many others were hidden. Their odds were going down by the second.

"Hey." The leader gestured to his men. "Go help Señor Botero out of his car."

Sean closed his fist around the butt of the gun in his pocket. "Don't make a move," he said. "Mr. Botero can't walk. We've already been through this. You deal with me."

"I think you are missing an important part of this meeting, Señor Driver. You are not in charge. Señor Botero is not in charge." The man grinned.

Sean noticed the scar above his brow. It was Sophie's masked man. His pulse sped up.

"I am in charge," the man said, kicking the fender again.

Sean's muscles were screaming for action. He clamped his jaw and forced himself to breathe normally.

"Get out of the car, old man!" The scarred man nodded to one of his men. The man lifted his weapon and started for the car.

Sean heard the back door open.

*Sophie, no!* What the hell was she doing? She couldn't talk, couldn't show her face. They'd know immediately that she wasn't Botero.

"Give me a minute."

The guttural whisper was quiet, but somehow it carried in the empty warehouse. And it sounded authentic. It could have been the voice of a frail, weak old man.

The gunman hesitated.

For an instant, nobody moved, then the raspy voice spoke again.

"Where is my daughter?"

The scarred man turned and aimed his gun at the open limo door. "Stop stalling. We can take the money any time we want." He laughed. "You came alone, just like you said you would."

"The cash is in the trunk," Sean said.

"Of course. That is the only place big enough to hold it. Or do you have a trap set for us there?"

"No trap," Sean said. He pressed the remote trunk release and the large black trunk opened.

"My daughter!" Sophie rasped.

"Shut up, old man. You'll never see your daughter alive."

"Fuentes!"

The voice came from behind Sean and to his right. He angled his head.

"Fuentes! *En el coche. Ese no es Botero!*"

Sean understood. *That's not Botero.* Before he could react, a rifle shot rang out, followed immediately by the pop of a bullet hitting steel.

He ducked and pulled his weapon. "Sophie! Get down!" Dear God, if she was hurt—

The three pickup men crouched and began firing. Sean fired back blindly. The air was filled with the zing and pop of bullets.

Gunfire exploded from the limo. It was Sophie. She wasn't hit!

The rifle fired again.

Sean took a deep breath and stood, turning to fire several shots in the direction of the rifleman. He heard a grunt. *Good.*

Then something knocked him sideways. He whirled. One of the three gunmen went down.

*Sophie.*

He got off a couple of quick shots and ducked back down behind the car. He tried to move backward, so he could get a glimpse of Sophie. But something was wrong. He pushed himself up to get another shot off, but he felt heavy, slow.

More shots rang out from the backseat of the limo.

The rifleman behind him fired again. The bullet ricocheted off the limousine's roof a few inches above his head.

He finally got to his feet, only to see the scarred man's gun barrel pointed directly at Sophie's head. Her gun was pointed at his midsection.

"Hold it," he growled, lifting his gun. His left hand was no help. In fact, he couldn't feel it, so he rested his wrist on the car top and leveled the gun at the scar on the man's right brow. "You can shoot her, but you will die."

From the corner of his eye, Sean thought he saw Sophie nudge the guy in the ribs. He smiled. "Where are your buddies?" he asked. What the hell was wrong with him? He could barely get enough breath to talk.

Sophie didn't move a muscle, except to shove the barrel of her gun into the scarred man's ribs again.

"They're down. Come on," she said to the man holding his gun to her head. "You don't want to die like your buddies, do you? We can make you a deal. You tell us where Sonya is, and we won't kill you. It's two against one."

Sean began to move around the front of the car. "Don't offer him a deal, Sophie. I want to kill him." It occurred to him that the reason he was moving slowly was that he'd been shot.

Once he was behind the scarred man, he stretched his right arm out and pressed the barrel of his gun to the man's head. "He killed Johnson. I'm ready to blow his head off."

The man stood without moving.

Sean knew if the murderer wanted to, he could get off a shot and kill Sophie by the time their bullets killed him. Sean prayed that the man wanted to live more than he wanted to kill Sophie.

It was a gamble. He knew she could identify him. He knew he was screwed, no matter what he did.

"Don't kill him yet," Sophie said. "I want to know who he is, and how he's involved with Sonya's kidnapping. That information could be worth a lot. Maybe even enough to cut him a deal, if he wants one."

"You don't want a deal, do you? I hope not." Sean cocked his gun.

The man flinched.

Sean held his breath.

"Okay," the man said. He opened his hand and let his gun drop.

The zing of a rifle shot echoed in Sean's ears, and at the same time, he heard sirens.

The scarred man hit the ground.

"In the car, Sophie!" Sean cried.

Without much hope, Sean shot toward the rifleman, emptying his magazine. Then he bent over the scarred man.

"Fuentes, Fuentes! That's your name isn't it?"

"Sonya—"

Sean grabbed a fistful of his shirt. "What about Sonya? Do you know where she is?"

The man coughed, and red bubbles spilled from his mouth. "Sonya—she's—"

Sirens screamed as an ambulance drove into the warehouse. Sean shouted to get them over to the scarred man. The EMTs jumped out and ran to the back to pull out a gurney.

"Listen to me Fuentes. Where is Sonya?"

More bubbles escaped the man's lips. He took a gurgling breath. "Ladera," he whispered. "Army base—" He coughed.

Sean nearly collapsed in relief. "Who are you working for?" he demanded.

The EMTs set down the gurney and bent over Fuentes. "This is bad," one said.

"How bad?"

"He took a high-powered bullet to his lung. We gotta get him on the road before he bleeds out."

Sean stood and a dark red haze crept into the edge of his vision. He swayed. "Don't let him die. He's got information that can save lives."

## Chapter Twelve

Rachel Brennan thanked the police commissioner for at least the fourth time, and said for at least the third time that she needed to hang up because she had a meeting.

She heard someone speak to him.

"Well, Rachel, I'm supposed to be in a meeting myself, so I'll let you go. Thank you again."

"Goodbye, sir." She jabbed the disconnect button and sighed audibly, then turned to the five people sitting at the big round table in her office.

"The police commissioner thanks us for our help in apprehending Craig Johnson's murderer."

"The person he should be thanking isn't here," Samantha said quietly.

"Sophie is at home. I had to force her to take a few days off. She's exhausted, after everything she's been through."

"Well, I'm glad the commissioner is pleased, but we still don't have Sonya Botero." Rafe appeared relaxed, but Rachel knew him. He was agitated. It showed in the way his fingers drummed on his thigh.

She smiled to herself as she glanced toward Isabelle, who had also picked up on Rafe's agitation. Isabelle had been watching him with a tiny frown ever since they'd sat down.

"The commissioner is aware of that, as am I," Rachel said, pacing across the room, playing with the cell phone she held. "But thanks to Sophie and Sean Majors, we now know that the man who knocked you down, Samantha, is the same man Sophie identified as riding the elevator with her the morning of Johnson's death, Unfortunately, he never made it to the hospital. He bled to death in the ambulance."

Rafe cursed in Spanish.

"Wait a minute, Rafe, before you turn the air blue with your language. His name was Jose Fuentes. He took a custodial job at the hospital several weeks ago. But the most important thing is, Sean was able to find out where Sonya is."

Rachel felt the tension in the room rise. She stopped pacing and crossed her arms.

"She's alive? I'm so glad." Behind her tortoiseshell glasses, Samantha's eyes filled with tears.

Julia Garcia made a small, gasping noise. Rachel smiled at her kindly and Samantha reached over and squeezed Julia's hand. Julia was Sonya's best friend, and Rachel understood how worried Julia had been.

"Where is she?" Rafe said, sitting up.

"I don't have a lot of specifics. Samantha, Julia, Ethan—that's all the information I have for you. Thanks for your hard work."

The three of them stood.

Isabelle and Rafe looked at Rachel questioningly.

"Rafe, Isabelle, please stay. I have something to discuss with you."

Once the others were gone, Rachel sat. She placed her cell phone on the table, then clasped her hands in front of her.

"What's going on, Rachel?" Rafe asked brusquely.

"Sean was only able to get three words out of Fuentes. 'Ladera,' and 'army base.'"

Rafe's dark eyes sparkled. "There are only a few army bases—no more than four or five. But they're all up in the mountains."

"I knew you'd have that information. Do you know where they are?"

He shook his head. "No, but I can find out." He dug in his pocket for his cell phone.

"Wait." Rachel stopped him with her hand. She turned to Isabelle, who was still watching Rafe guardedly. Rachel considered them. She'd wondered if they were dating, but a bit of careful investigation had told her they weren't. Still, the sparks were there. The heat in any room went up several degrees whenever they were together.

It was ironic that Isabelle was the perfect Confidential agent to accompany Rafe to Ladera. For a few seconds earlier this morning, when she'd made the decision to send them, she'd debated whether it was a good idea to throw them together in such dangerous and emotionally charged circumstances. But ultimately, she'd made her decision, as she always did, based on the facts. Emotion didn't enter in. If it entered into *their* relationship, that was their business.

"Rafe, you've lived in South America. You know the areas, as well as the drug trade, intimately."

She turned to Isabelle, whose eyes were wide with wary expectation. "Isabelle, as spokeswoman for Weddings Your Way, it will make perfect sense for you to travel to Ladera. You'll be doing damage control. You will make statements to the local press assuring them that the DeLeon-Botero wedding is still on. You will also meet with Juan DeLeon's family and reassure them that Sonya will be found safe and sound."

Isabelle stared at her. "I can't go with *him*."

"What?" Rafe leaned forward. "Why not? I think it's a great idea."

Rachel didn't say anything. She stood.

"But Rachel, if I'm there with him, everyone will think—"

"Exactly. It's a beautiful plan," Rafe said. "You will keep the locals occupied with your press conferences and appearances while I search for Sonya."

"You're not going to leave me to answer all the questions alone. I want to find Sonya as much as you do."

Rachel slipped out the door of her office and headed downstairs to tell Vicki to make airline and hotel reservations.

Sparks were flying, all right. She hoped she'd made the right choice about who to send.

SOPHIE POURED A CUP of coffee and wandered around her living room. There were still a few strips of crime-scene tape dangling from doorknobs and shelves, and the whole place was littered with fingerprint backing strips.

She leaned over to pick up a couple, but her hand hurt and her head felt woozy.

She hadn't slept a wink all night. She'd tried listening to music, reading, taking a hot bath, even drinking warm milk. Nothing had helped. Every time she closed her eyes, she saw Sean with blood spreading across his white T-shirt as the paramedics urged him to lie down. It was the first time anyone realized he'd been shot.

After Jose Fuentes had dropped his weapon, things happened so fast that she'd been dazed.

She should have known he was hurt. She'd sat there in the backseat of the limousine while he'd leaned on the door. If she'd dared to look closely enough, if she'd had the courage to speak to him, she'd have known something was wrong.

But she'd been too cowardly and too selfish. She hadn't wanted to face the scorn she was sure she'd see in his eyes.

He'd been right about her all along. She was too much like his ex-wife. He'd said he wasn't a good judge of women, and she had to admit he was right.

Then, once she'd realized he'd been shot, she'd backed away even more. Seeing him hurt and vulnerable, seeing how close he'd come to dying, had forced her to confront an awful truth.

She loved him.

It was stupid. It was fruitless. And it was her own fault. She'd let him in. But none of that made one bit of difference.

She was in love with him. She had no idea how she could live without him. And *that* was what had kept her from sleeping.

She sat down at her little table and looked at the clock—9:00 a.m. He'd probably been up since six, had breakfast with Michaela, dressed, gone by the hospital to check on Carlos, then to the police station to sign his statements.

"Oh, Sophie, stop it," she told herself sternly. She couldn't spend her days thinking about what he was doing. He was gone. Out of her life. He and Michaela.

Something splashed on her hand. She looked down, then realized she was crying.

"This is why you never date," she reminded herself, sniffling and wiping her eyes. "This is why—" She sobbed.

*Oh, she was pathetic.*

Her doorbell rang.

She jumped, and spilled coffee on the table. Who would be at her door?

It was probably the police. She'd meant to check in with Rachel this morning before she went down to the station to sign her statement. She wanted to make sure she didn't give out too much information about Confidential.

She'd just tell the detective she'd talk to him later. She stood and looked down at herself. She had on cotton pajama bottoms and a tank top. As she went to the door, she grabbed a light cotton zippered sweater to cover her arms.

Peeking through the peephole, she couldn't see anything. She opened the door cautiously.

"Sean!"

He stood there, in jeans and the frayed Miami Heat T-shirt she'd seen before, looking heartbreakingly handsome, and surprisingly fit for someone who'd been shot.

"Can I come in?" he asked.

Her fingers wouldn't work for a few seconds, then she finally grabbed the doorknob and pulled the door open far enough to let him in.

As he walked by her, she got a whiff of woods, citrus and him. The scent swirled around her like a ghostly embrace. She sniffed quietly and patted her cheeks with one hand.

He turned, and she realized he didn't look as well as she'd first thought. His mouth was pinched and white at the corners, and there was an irregular bulge under the T-shirt between his shoulder and his neck. A bandage.

"Are you okay?" she asked.

He nodded, not meeting her eyes. "Sure. Just a flesh wound. You?"

"Of course. I'm fine." She stood there for a few seconds, hugging herself and looking at the neck of his T-shirt where the edge of the bandage stuck out.

"How is—"

"Can I—"

They both spoke at the same time. Sean smiled and gestured for her to go first.

She gave a tiny shrug. "I just wondered how Carlos is."

His smile faded. "He's all right, but he can't take

much more of this. None of the strokes have been major, but he's losing strength. I'm afraid he's losing hope."

"He can't. We *will* find Sonya."

He nodded. "Got any more of that coffee?"

She took a deep breath. "Sure." Brushing past him, she grabbed a mug and filled it, then stared down into it, realizing how little she really knew about him. Except that he was honorable and decent. He loved his daughter more than anything, and he'd made love to her as if he'd loved her.

"I don't know what you like in your coffee," she said sadly.

"Nothing."

She held out the mug.

He took it in his right hand. "Thanks."

What was he doing here? He didn't seem to want to talk, or maybe he was as uncomfortable as she was.

"Did you need to tell me something?"

He took a sip of his coffee, then looked up at her from under his brows. "Yeah."

She waited, but he just stood there, drinking his coffee.

"I guess Rachel filled you in on the Confidential Agency."

He nodded.

"Look, Sean. I'm sorry about all that. I'm sworn—"

He banged the coffee cup down on the table.

She jumped and backed away until her hips pressed against the counter.

"Damn it, Sophie," he muttered. "I didn't mean to scare you."

She crossed her arms and pressed them against her middle. "What do you want?"

He stood there, too close, for a moment, while she kept her eyes on the *A* in the word HEAT on his T-shirt. It was all she could do to keep from crying. If she looked at him, at his teal blue eyes, at his mouth that was just a little crooked when he smiled, she'd break down. She thought about pushing him aside and running out of her apartment, but that wouldn't be a permanent solution. She'd have to come back eventually.

"It wasn't really my idea to come here."

Hope that she hadn't even known was there dissolved, like an ice cube in boiling water. Quickly, totally, painfully.

"It was—"

She closed her eyes and waited.

A soft touch on her chin surprised her. His finger, pressing, urging her chin up.

"Look at me, Sophie."

She opened her eyes, humiliated that they were wet.

"Michaela wants to see you."

"M-M-Mi—?" She couldn't even talk. She sniffled.

He nodded, his face solemn, his eyes as blue as the sea. "She wants to play bounce on Sophie. I told her I'd ask if you wanted to."

Sophie couldn't stop the tears that poured down her cheeks. She had no idea what Sean was talking about. Her thoughts and emotions were all mixed up.

"It won't work," she said finally, turning her back on

him and pressing her palms down on the cool counter-top. She squeezed her eyes shut. "You were right in the first place. I am just like your ex-wife. I'm worse. I did drugs. I—I didn't know I was pregnant, but still." Her breaths were coming short and shallow. She covered her mouth for a moment, trying to regain control. "Your wife may have abandoned Michaela, but at least she left her safe with you. I abandoned my baby in the worst way. I killed her."

She knew that would stop Sean, and it did. He didn't say anything for a long time. She felt him behind her. Heard him breathing.

"Is that what you think? That you killed your baby?"

"What would you call it? I let my boyfriend talk me into using drugs, and my baby died."

"You told me you had a miscarriage. Is that true?"

She nodded.

"You were seventeen. A child yourself."

She buried her face in her hands.

"How far along were you?"

How much more could she take? Not much. "I didn't know I was pregnant. Maybe a few weeks." Her voice was muffled by her hands.

"Have you done drugs since?"

She shook her head.

He touched her shoulder, then squeezed gently. "You hadn't been with a man since either, had you, until the other night?"

She jerked away from his touch and turned around. "How much more do you want to know?" she demanded. "How many times we did it? How long I did drugs?

What I do for fun these days?" Her jaw hurt, her eyes burned, and she had to stop this. She adored Michaela, but she couldn't afford to become any more attached to her. It would hurt too much to be so close to him.

"You already know that my real mother abandoned me, that the woman who raised me beat me, and of course I let my own child die. What else can I tell you?"

His eyes turned stormy. "I'm trying to make a point," he said impatiently. "But apparently you're too filled with self-pity right now to think straight."

She gaped at him.

"Are you angry now? Good. Because I don't like you when you're feeling sorry for yourself." He grabbed her hand and when she tried to pull away, he squeezed it more tightly.

"Now listen to me. I was wrong about you. I think I knew that from the beginning. I was just feeling sorry for myself and making excuses."

She pulled against his grip again, but he was relentless.

"Stop it. I want to hold your hand and look into your eyes while I say this. Sophie Brooks, I think you are the most beautiful thing I've ever seen. And the second most stubborn, after my daughter. Maybe third. Rosita is pretty stubborn, too."

Sophie couldn't help but smile.

Sean pulled her closer and let go of her hand, only to slip his arm around her. She put her hands against his chest—hands that trembled.

"My daughter and my housekeeper seem to think that they'd like to have you around."

"I thought you were trying to make a point," Sophie said. "Will we be getting to it anytime within, say, the next five years?"

He smiled his crooked smile and leaned down and kissed her. His mouth was hot and firm. He tasted of coffee, and his kiss sent little erotic thrills all the way through her.

When he lifted his head, she reached for his mouth with hers, so he kissed her again, then pushed the sweater down her arms and trailed his lips and tongue down her neck and along her shoulder to the curve and farther, to the bad scar. He kissed it and made it better.

Sophie threw her head back, and he kissed her throat and the underside of her chin. "Do you even know how beautiful and brave and special you are?" he whispered against her skin.

"Sean, please stop. I'm no good at this. I don't think I can have a casual relationship—"

He put his finger against her lips. "Exactly the point I was trying to make. Sophie, do think you might consider marrying me?"

*Marriage.* She blinked away the haze of desire and stared at him. "I never thought I'd get married."

Sean nibbled on her ear. "I hear it's all the rage," he whispered.

"I've never been one to follow fashion." Her calm words didn't reflect how she was feeling inside. Her stomach was fluttering, her pulse was racing, and she had the strangest urge to laugh out loud.

Sean looked her in the eye. "Someone told me the groom likes long black silky stockings."

The laughter burst forth, free and light and healing. "Long black stockings? Those are so hot, especially in the summer. I think I may be wearing long swishy dresses and cool linen pants from now on."

"You could always save the black stockings for the bedroom."

Sophie's cheeks burned, and Sean smiled and kissed her as he ran his hand up her waist under the tank top until his warm fingers touched the underside of her breast. "Now, speaking of bedrooms, where's yours? The groom is impatient to get started on the honeymoon."

Sophie pulled away and glared at him. "You don't think you fooled me, do you, Mr. Security Chief? You've been in my bedroom, snooping around. You know exactly where it is."

His blue eyes sparkled as he smiled. "That's right. I do." And with a wink, he took her hand to lead the way into their future.

\* \* \* \* \*

*Don't miss the gripping conclusion of*
*MIAMI CONFIDENTIAL*
*next month when Dana Marton presents*
BRIDAL OP
*only from Harlequin Intrigue.*

# SAVE UP TO $30! SIGN UP TODAY!

INSIDE Romance

The complete guide to your favorite
Harlequin®, Silhouette® and Love Inspired® books.

✓ Newsletter ABSOLUTELY FREE! No purchase necessary.

✓ Valuable coupons for future purchases of Harlequin,
  Silhouette and Love Inspired books in every issue!

✓ Special excerpts & previews in each issue. Learn about all
  the hottest titles before they arrive in stores.

✓ No hassle—mailed directly to your door!

✓ Comes complete with a handy shopping checklist
  so you won't miss out on any titles.

- - - - - - - - - - - - - - - - - - - - - - - - - - - - - - - - - -

## SIGN ME UP TO RECEIVE INSIDE ROMANCE
## ABSOLUTELY FREE
*(Please print clearly)*

Name

Address

City/Town                    State/Province                    Zip/Postal Code

(098 KKM EJL9)

**Please mail this form to:**
In the U.S.A.: Inside Romance, P.O. Box 9057, Buffalo, NY 14269-9057
In Canada: Inside Romance, P.O. Box 622, Fort Erie, ON L2A 5X3
OR visit http://www.eHarlequin.com/insideromance

IRNBPA06R        ® and ™ are trademarks owned and used by the trademark owner and/or its licensee.

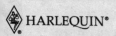

If you enjoyed what you just read,
then we've got an offer you can't resist!

# Take 2 bestselling love stories FREE!

# Plus get a FREE surprise gift!

**Hidden in the secrets of antiquity,
lies the unimagined truth...**

Introducing

ROGUE
Angel™

a brand-new line filled with mystery
and suspense, action and adventure,
and a fascinating look into history.

**And it all begins with DESTINY.**

In a sealed crypt in
France, where the
terrifying legend of
the beast of Gevaudan
begins to unravel,
Annja Creed discovers
a stunning artifact
that will seal her destiny.

*Available every other
month starting
July 2006, wherever
you buy books.*

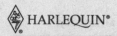

# HARLEQUIN®

## American ROMANCE®

# American Beauties

### SORORITY SISTERS,
### FRIENDS FOR LIFE

# Michele Dunaway

# THE MARRIAGE CAMPAIGN

Campaign fund-raiser Lisa Meyer has worked
hard to be her own boss and will let nothing—
especially romance—interfere with her success.
To Mark Smith, Lisa is the perfect candidate for
him to spend his life with. But if she lets herself
fall for Mark, will she lose all she's worked for?
Or will she have a future that's more than
she's ever dreamed of?

**On sale August 2006**

Also watch for:

## THE WEDDING SECRET
**On sale December 2006**

## NINE MONTHS NOTICE
**On sale April 2007**

*Available wherever Harlequin books are sold.*

**www.eHarlequin.com**

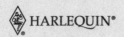

# HARLEQUIN®

# INTRIGUE®

## COMING NEXT MONTH

### #933 BRIDAL OP by Dana Marton
*Miami Confidential*

Weddings Your Way agents Isabelle Rush and Rafe Montoya are sent to exotic Ladera to save a kidnapping victim, but when politicians and hired guns converge on the hot spot, passion won't be the only thing that erupts.

### #934 THE HIDDEN HEIR by Debra Webb
*Colby Agency*

Ashley Orrick has gone to extraordinary lengths to keep anyone from finding her and her son. But when Colby agent Keith Devers catches up with her, can she trust him to believe her story when no one else will?

### #935 BEAUTIFUL BEAST by Dani Sinclair

When an explosion ended Gabriel Lowe's military career and left him scarred, his life became a shadow of what it once was. But the beautiful Cassiopia Richards is determined to warm this beast's heart before an old enemy cuts short both their futures.

### #936 UNDENIABLE PROOF by B.J. Daniels
*Cape Diablo*

Witness to a murder, Willa St. Clair seeks safety on a secluded island in the Gulf of Mexico. But when a group of killers picks up on her trail, undercover cop Landry Jones arrives to protect her, if the evils of Cape Diablo don't get them all first.

### #937 VOW TO PROTECT by Ann Voss Peterson
*Wedding Mission*

Cord Turner never knew his father was serial killer Dryden Kane. He never knew he had twin sisters, or that former love Melanie Frist was pregnant with his son. So when Kane escapes police custody, Cord's sure going to have one heck of a family reunion.

### #938 DAKOTA MELTDOWN by Elle James

When hometown girl Brenna Jensen is called in to investigate a potential killer, she's forced to collaborate with hardheaded FBI agent Nick Tarver. But as the winter ice thaws around Riverton, dead bodies surface, and the two of them are going to have to get along quickly if they're to survive the oncoming deluge.